P9-EMP-744

BY

THE

TIME

YOU

READ

THIS,

I'LL

BE

DEAD

BY THE TIME YOU READ THIS, I'LL BE DEAD

———————

JULIE ANNE PETERS

HYPERION
NEW YORK

If you purchased this book without a cover, you should be aware
that this book is stolen property. It was reported as "unsold and
destroyed" to the publisher, and neither the author nor the publisher
has received any payment for this "stripped" book.

Text copyright © 2010 by Julie Anne Peters
All rights reserved. Published by Hyperion, an imprint of Disney
Book Group. No part of this book may be reproduced or transmitted
in any form or by any means, electronic or mechanical, including
photocopying, recording, or by any information storage and retrieval
system, without written permission from the publisher.
For information address Hyperion,
114 Fifth Avenue, New York, New York 10011-5690.

Printed in the United States of America
First Hyperion paperback edition, 2011
10 9 8 7 6 5 4 3 2 1
V475-2873-0-11060

Designed by Elizabeth H. Clark
ISBN 978-1-4231-3021-5
Visit www.hyperionteens.com

To C. J. Bott
for her tireless campaign against bullying

BY
THE
TIME
YOU
READ
THIS,
I'LL
BE
DEAD

- 23 DAYS -

The white boy, the skinny, tall boy with shocking white hair, sneaks behind the stone bench and leans against the tree trunk. Since I can't move my head, I watch him out of the corner of my eye. He could be a ghost. For a minute I think he's here to contact me, but that would be stupid. I don't see dead people.

He pulls out a paperback and starts reading.

I hunch over my own book.

Mom's black CR-V crunches to the curb and idles. I rip out the page I just read, ball it in my fist, and stand.

The white boy watches me. I don't make eye contact. Not with him. Not with anyone.

I shoulder my book bag, walk to the car, open the door, and get in. My thighs squeeze together.

"Who is that?" Mom asks. She's peering over my shoulder at the white boy. In the side-view mirror, I see he's moved to the bench and taken my spot. Like he did yesterday.

"Was he talking to you? Do you know him?"

He's into me, Mom. He likes ugly sick girls who have to wear neck braces.

She shifts into drive. "I don't want you associating with people outside of school, people I don't know. If anyone talks to you, go back inside the building."

What if I talk to *them?*

That was a joke.

She checks the rearview mirror to merge into the street. Her face is filled with worry lines. "Your father has a late meeting with a client, so it'll just be us for dinner."

She smiles expectantly.

I can't even look at her.

"I'll be leaving for Houston in the morning, but I shouldn't have to stay more than two days. Dad will drive you to school and pick you up. He may be a few minutes late if he can't get away by two thirty, but you just wait for him on the bench." We circle the roundabout and she adds, "If that . . . person, if anyone bothers you, tell your dad."

Sure, Mom. I'll use sign language.

Wal-Mart, on my right, is packed. "Oh, I really need to stop for deodorant and toothpaste." She slows at the entrance, but doesn't turn in. We pass the Wal-Mart. "Never mind. I'll get them on my way to the airport."

Her eyes betray the fear. She'll never lose it. She doesn't stop because she's afraid I'll have a wack attack. I've only had one in public, but it happened when she left me alone in the car. It was in our red car, the old one. I was ten. She needed to pick up a few groceries at King Soopers on our way home from school. She said a few. I had to go to the bathroom, but I figured a few meant a few minutes. She said, "I'll be right back." She said that: "Right. Back."

4

The door shut and instantly all the air in the car compressed. I couldn't breathe. Minutes ticked by. The walls closed in. She left me there, alone, and I knew, I just knew she was never coming back for me. My bladder ballooned like I'd been guzzling water for weeks, and even when I crossed my legs and scrunched up tight, I couldn't hold it.

At the first dribble, I squealed. Then I exploded. I don't remember screaming or honking the horn. The fear of being locked inside, I remember every day. If I close my eyes, I can hear the ringing in my ears, still, from the blaring horn. I see the distorted faces of everyone peering through the window. Mom's panicked eyes. The door unlocking and her hand wrenching mine away from the horn.

"What's the matter?" she cries.

I heave a sob. "I peed my pants." The stretchy pink capris she just got me. Ruined.

Mom gives me that look, like, Who are you? *What* are you?

She has to tell the people, "It's nothing. She's fine. I was only gone a few minutes."

People leave.

She's humiliated.

"Why did you do that?" she said between clenched teeth as we drove away fast. She was powerless to control me. She still is. I was trapped, Mom. Why don't you *get* that?

Peeing my pants isn't the reason she can't leave me alone now. I'm under twenty-four-hour suicide watch.

If I could speak, I'd tell her, "What can happen in a few minutes changes you forever."

- 2 2 DAYS -

I found Through-the-Light by accident. I don't normally believe in accidents. Divine intervention, maybe. Except I don't believe in God. I want to. I just can't. There's a higher power guiding me, for sure, because it guided me to Through-the-Light.

I don't remember what I was searching for on the Web. Suicide. Death. Wills. That was it. Wills. I wanted to write a will. It wouldn't be legal or anything, since I'm not eighteen. I just thought a will would be less personal than a suicide note. Less . . . upsetting.

www.Through-the-Light.com popped up on my screen.

My eyes were drawn to the bits and pieces of description: *assist completers . . . if your time is now . . . may not discourage or dissuade . . . self-termination is your right.*

I *had* to choose it, maximize the window. Through-the-Light is a site where people will themselves away. That's the only way to explain it. You don't have to pay and you don't fill out forms to make it legal. Who cares about legalities when you're dead?

The home page is black and white. No frills. No flashing ads. That attracted me. When you enter, your monitor goes completely blank, then this white, burning light almost blinds you. If you look hard, and don't look away, you see the message:

Are you ready to pass Through-the-Light?

I'd been ready my whole life.

The default answer is *No*.

I tabbed to *Yes*.

A pop-up box appeared and I was asked to sign this privacy policy, which I didn't read all the way through at the time. I should have. The last paragraph ended, *By agreeing to the terms of this site, you release Through-the-Light of all responsibility for your actions.*

Agree? *No Yes*

I clicked my mouse pointer on *Yes*.

Please press dominant index finger to screen.

Why? I thought. Weird, but I did it.

Please wait.

I swore I felt heat through my skin.

Do you agree to the minimum and maximum time limits?

Yes No

Whatever. I wanted in.

I chose *Yes*.

Thank you, Daelyn Rice.

What? How did it know my name?

Your ID is J_Doe071894.

Which was eerie. July 18, 1994 is my birthday. Dad must've set up a profile for me on this computer and not secured it. Stupid. Everyone who's registered or accepted by Through-the-Light is J_Doe something. Anonymous, genderless.

There were three selections on the main menu: *DOD*, *FF*, *WTG*.

I didn't know what they meant.

Start at the beginning, I figured. I moved my pointer to *DOD* and clicked. A message popped up.

Touch screen activated.

My new PC has a touch screen. When my parents gave me back my computer privileges, they surprised me with this new PC. Parentally controlled, of course. I'd used touch screens on the kiosks at King Soopers and Wally World. I pressed my right index finger on *DOD* and a list appeared.

J_Doe092854

J_Doe031392

J_Doe102385 . . .

Eight people. Or members. Or pulses of light.

The monitor went blank for a second and a large, italicized message filled the screen.

Your Date of Determination will be 23 days from today. Will you be prepared, Daelyn Rice? No Yes

Twenty-three days? That was too long. I was ready now. I touched *No.*

Enter DOD _____.

I entered tomorrow's date, but it came back *Invalid Entry.* I tried the day after. A message appeared:

Policy states DOD minimum is 23 days.

Twenty-three days was too long. I could've just backed

out, closed the window. But I didn't. I felt somehow that Through-the-Light had found me, had known my true desire. I touched *Default*. The earliest possible date appeared: April 24.

That seemed forever away.

The DOD list reappeared, scrolling down my screen. DOD. Date of Determination. These people must've reached their day, I figured out.

Lucky them.

White Boy is green today. His shirt is green, anyway. A logo tee, which I can't read from this distance. Cream khakis, which would make him look nerdy if they weren't wrinkled and over-long. He raises his eyes from his book and locks them on me as I open the gate, exit, and shut the gate behind me.

I'm not really looking. His bleached-out hair is gelled in spikes.

The stone bench is gray. The grass is gray. My life is dirty gray.

I pull out *Desire in the Mist*. *Chapter eighteen*, I read silently.

Maggie Louise knew from the look on Charles's face that she'd said the wrong thing. "Charles—"

He held up a hand. "No, Maggie Louise. I won't stand in the way of your happiness. If you love this man—"

A blur of body mass causes me to blink and lose my place.

He hip-hop dances in front of me. Skip-jumps back and forth.

First of all, he sucks.

Second, leave me alone.

I resume reading.

Maggie Louise had never known a man who'd give up his happiness for her. And she was his whole happiness. She'd been his wife for four years, his lover before that, his friend and ally. She wished now they'd adopted the Russian child. Or the Vietnamese one. She wished she wasn't leaving him alone.

Maggie Louise is me, in my next life. If I get a second chance.

The sound of pounding feet grabs my attention again. He krumps past me. "Ow," he says, grabbing his upper arm. "I think I dislocated my shoulder."

He's not funny.

"When do you want me to leave, Maggie Louise?" Charles asked.

She wasn't prepared to give him a date. She hesitated. She studied the man who'd been her constant companion, her champion and friend. Charles, oh, Charles. She didn't want to lose him, but what choice did she have?

Blocking my light, Green Boy stands there, waiting.

He dusts off his other shoulder.

Inwardly, I roll my eyes.

"Aha!" He points.

He didn't see that. He's making fun of me. Jerk.

Dad pulls up to the curb and I rip out page 181. Balling it in my fist, I throw it at the boy.

"Your mother is in Houston. Her plane set down around noon. She wanted me to let you know she arrived safely."

Because that is a grave concern.

Dad says, "How was your day?"

Eventful, actually. White boys can't dance. Also, two girls—two Catholic School girls—shared a joint in the john while I was changing my tampon. I sat on the toilet as long as I could, inhaling their secondhand smoke. You probably couldn't die from huffing pot, but hope springs eternal.

My butt got numb, so I stood and flushed. They yelped. They were fanning the air as I emerged from the stall. For a second I thought they were dispersing the stink of my presence. One went, "Shit. It's that weird deaf chick."

The other elbowed her.

Dumb, I wanted to say. Not deaf. Dumb. Make that stupid, like you.

"You won't rat us out, will you?" the elbower asked.

The mean girl clicked her tongue. "She can't talk."

Right, I thought. I'm deaf.

I needed to wash my hands. To get to the sink, I'd have to squeeze by one or both of them. Which would mean human contact.

"Damn. That was a waste of good weed." Intellectually-challenged-socially-aware-and-sensitive girl blew on her soggy joint.

I inched past her, punched the hand blower with my elbow (like, blow-dry your joint, hello?), then left.

"She's so freaking weird," I heard the mean girl say.

Twenty-two days, I thought. I held my hands up in the air the way surgeons do on TV, fingers spread. The other restroom on this floor was for faculty only. Thank the Virgin Mary it wasn't locked.

I scrubbed and scrubbed with hand soap. As the water

11

diluted my filth, all the air in my lungs expelled. What if I'd gotten menstrual blood on me?

I really was a sick person.

"She'll be home by Friday," Dad says.

I switch back to the present.

He massages his neck. "Is it okay with you if we just order takeout? I don't feel like cooking."

Then don't. I focus on the road, the path ahead.

I should clarify. The restrictions on my 24/7 suicide watch have been relaxed. I can be trusted to go to school, and to wait on a bench. A year has passed since my last failure. Not attempt. Failure.

Dad reaches over and cranks up the volume on the CD he's playing. It's techno, for God's sake. My stomach hurts from cramps anyway, but that music makes me want to hurl.

I think he thinks it'll make him seem cool.

News you can use, Dad. Losers aren't cool.

He orders one of those family combos with wonton soup, egg rolls, sweet and sour shrimp, Kung Pao chicken, Hunan beef, steamed rice, and fried rice. It's enough food to feed all the starving children in Africa.

It smells good, but it looks like doggie doo now that it's liquefied in the blender. I can no longer eat real food. This is God's idea of irony.

Dad says, "I'm going to watch the news. You can watch with me or, if you want, you can eat in your room."

See? Major leap of faith.

He'll still check on me periodically. He'll find excuses

to walk by my room or open and close the hall closet.

From my bedroom door in the middle of the hall, I slowly turn. Dad is watching me. I throw him a bone—eye contact. Catch.

He says, "I'm glad you're here, Daelyn."

The shrink told him to say that. I duck into my room.

Sitting at my desk, I flash back to the audition when I was seven. Dad read about this talent agency that was coming to town looking for child actors. "Singing and dancing ability a plus," he read to me. I told him, "I can't dance." He said, "But you sing like an angel."

He'd heard me singing along to a TV show, and the next thing I knew I was singing solo because Dad had remoted down the sound. "You're really good," he said. "Maybe even better than your mother. Don't tell her I said that." He winked. That made me happy because Mom had a beautiful voice. Wherever we drove, Dad would play CDs from films and musicals and encourage me to sing along. "You're going to be the next American Idol," he said.

I beamed. I actually believed him.

The audition was held in a huge auditorium that was packed with kids and parents. I wore my best dress, the one with puffy sleeves and sparkles. Looking at all those people . . . . The thought of getting up in front of them and singing . . .

I whispered to Dad, "I don't want to do this. Can we go home?"

"You'll be great." He squeezed my hand. "Just pretend you're singing in the car."

"Dad," I said urgently, "I don't want to."

13

He wouldn't listen.

He doesn't listen. No one ever listened to me.

I was assigned a number: 203. By the time my number was called, it was late afternoon and my stomach was growling with hunger and twisted in knots. Dad said, "Now don't be nervous. Just answer their questions and speak up. Then sing the way you do for me." He smiled and pushed me onstage.

I don't remember the questions. I sang "Somewhere Over the Rainbow" like a hundred kids had before me. My voice shook, but I didn't forget the lyrics, and I hit all the high notes.

A deep voice from the audience reverberated: "Thank you. You have a nice voice, but we're not looking for your type." I turned to leave, but Dad walked out onstage. "What type?"

When there was no answer, Dad repeated the question. "What type?" He sounded mad.

The deep voice sounded: "Do I have to say it?"

"Yes," Dad said. "What do you mean her 'type'?"

There was a hushed silence in the auditorium.

I felt all hot and flushed. Don't say it, I thought. Not out loud.

The voice boomed. "In case you hadn't noticed, your daughter is . . . overweight."

People's snickers and snorts drifted up to me.

Dad didn't say, "No, she's not." Because he knew I was and he made me humiliate myself in public.

I take my poo poo platter smoothie to the bed.

That was ages ago, but it sticks in my mind as a turning point. I'd never trust my dad again.

14

- 21 DAYS -

*It only requires a fingerprint match to sign on to Through-the-*Light. Excellent technology.

Welcome J_Doe071894.

I touch *DOD*.

Five today. Five new IDs. I don't know why, but I wonder how many are—were—girls. I read somewhere that more guys commit suicide than girls. Girls talk about it. Girls attempt it. Boys do it. I calculate how old each was. 22, 18, 30, 46, 15—my age.

How did they do it? When? Like, what time? Morning, afternoon? I want to go in the morning. Give myself time. Time to get dead and stay dead.

I touch *FF*.

A familiar screen appears. A discussion board. I live on discussion boards, in chat rooms and bully boards. I write stories about how people verbally assault me every day of my life and how adults don't care and even contribute to the abuse. People on boards are always sympathetic, but they don't really care about me, either. They're just there for themselves.

Welcome to the Final Forum. Use this board to communicate with others who are completers. Please note: Participants may not attempt to dissuade or discourage self-termination. Disregard for free will and informed consent will result in immediate removal from the board. Future access to Through-the-Light will be denied. This board is monitored at all times.

That's comforting. I've been to suicide boards before where people get on and say stuff like, "Don't do it. Suicide is not the answer."

They don't know the question.

Or, "Life's a bitch. Get used to it."

Thanks.

"Suicide is the easy way out."

If it's so easy, why am I still here?

And my favorite: "God loves you. Life is the most precious gift from God. You will break God's heart if you throw His gift away."

God has a heart? That's news to me.

People on boards can be very, very shallow.

The Final Forum has a long list of topics, including: *Random Rants, Bullied, Divorce, Disease, So Tired, Hate This Life, Bleak, Bequests, Attempts.*

Already I like this board.

I start with *Random Rants.*

The future holds no hope or meaning to me. I know that by killing myself other people will suffer, but why go through this interminable hell? What's the point of being here if you feel unloved and abandoned by those you used to trust and count on? What's the point of living if you don't belong anywhere?

So true.

The next entry.

I'm nothing. I'm no one. I'm gone.

Poetic. But I'm not philosophical about life. I skip to *Bullied.*

J_Doe032692 wrote: *I am not a thin person. However, this does not give people the right to make fun of me* every day. *This does not give people the right to taunt me, calling me ugly and worthless, telling me to kill myself because no one will ever want me, or to make up songs about why I am so fat and how much food I eat. NO ONE. I repeat, NO ONE HAS THE RIGHT TO HURT ANOTHER HUMAN BEING THIS BADLY.*

My throat constricts. The neck brace feels as if it's shrinking and cutting off my esophagus. I reach up to cover the words with my hand and the Web site dissolves.

I want to go. Now.

When Dad drops me off he doesn't say anything about picking me up early. I bet he'd like to leave me and never come back. I wonder if Mom even told him I have a half day today. All he says is, "I love you, honey."

He has to say that.

It's windy. I hate wind. Goose pimples prickle my bare legs, and I will them away. Don't engage your senses. Don't feel, don't touch, taste, hear, speak.

No one tries to engage me all morning, which isn't unusual. My econ teacher smiles, but she has to. She's a nun. It's obvious by the way my teachers avoid me or look at me like I'm a freak that they know my history. Thanks, Mom and Dad. No doubt they told the principal, who talked to all my teachers, who now condemn or pity me.

"Hey, you're out early. What is it, Debutante Day?" Green Boy plops down next to me on the bench. Too close. My arms press to my sides.

He inches closer.

I shoot him a fiery glare.

"Yikes!" He slides back an inch. "If you want me to go, just say so."

I don't because I can't. I'd move if there was any other place to sit near the loading zone. Anyway, I was here first.

He sprawls, his legs extending straight out and his hands locking behind his head. "Hygrometer rising. Upslope conditions and a high-pressure ridge with that plume of tropical moisture typically means monsoonal flow from the Gulf. Smell it?"

I don't smell.

"Smells like rain. With a little skunk mixed in."

I catch a glimpse of his face. His smile. He wiggles his dark eyebrows and I shrink to try and make myself invisible.

Go away.

"I'm Santana, by the way." One of his arms flies in front of my face, fingers spread. I flinch. He waits a second, then raises and lowers his hand like he's checking if I'm zoned.

If he touches me . . .

I'll scream. I will. Or if I can't, I'll bite him.

"What you've heard is true." He does a thumbs-up. "The ladies love me."

I swing my knees to the right, over the end of the bench,

18

to turn my back on him. I retrieve *Desire in the Mist* from my book bag. The pages riffle in the wind and I hold them down.

"I live in that house next door." He waits. For what, I don't know. "I see you come here after school every day."

Is he watching me?

He adds, "Obviously looking for me."

When I don't respond, he says, "I did shower this morning. Passed through the decontamination chamber and everything."

I hunch over my book and concentrate hard. *Charles removed a suitcase from the closet shelf and opened it onto the bed. Maggie Louise watched from their bedroom door. Their bedroom, where they'd slept and talked long into the night and made love to the sounds of the city. Charles stopped suddenly and braced himself on the carved mahogany headboard. His shoulders began to shake*—

Green Boy says, "Okay, I confess. I'm a stalker."

He's irritating. I reach in my bag for a pen. In the bottom margin of my book, I write, "Why don't you just kill me now?" I rip out the page, swivel around on the bench, and thrust it at him.

He reads it. "I said stalker. Not strangler."

A moment passes. He smiles. "Did I mention the ladies love me?"

I bury my head in my book. *"Oh, love. My love."* Maggie *Louise rushed across*—

Green Boy sighs.

I think, Loser. In my peripheral vision, I see him look at me. Just stare at the side of my face or my neck brace. I wish he'd go I wish he'd go I wish—

He says, "May I ask what you're reading?" He reaches out to rotate the book toward him.

I clutch it to my chest, like a shield.

His arm retracts, but he angles his head over to read the cover. "Ah," he goes. "I read *Desire in the Mist* for comparative lit last year."

He is *so* not funny.

"My favorite part is where our heroine says to the studnut on the cover, 'You're the only man I've ever loved. The only man I ever will. And yet, I'd trade you in for a Gucci bag.'"

Shut up.

"'Oh, darling. My darling,'" Green Boy mocks in a falsetto. He falls off the bench onto his knees and steeples his hands. "'Just one more time, let me play your instrument of love.'"

"Sorry." His voice lowers to normal and he goes, "'I mean, your tremendous trombone of manhood.'"

The wind lifts my hair and I think, Take me away. I can't be feeling this, whatever it is. Interest? I stand to leave.

"Wait." He scrambles to his feet. "I'm not making fun of your reading tastes. You should see the crap I read."

My hair flies in front of my face.

Where's Dad? He's stranded me. I gaze down the street as if wishing will make Dad magically appear.

Green Boy extracts a tin from his front pocket. His long-sleeved shirt flaps in the wind as he opens the tin.

The scent of licorice tickles my nose. I blow out all smell.

"I bought this online at a classic candy store," he says. "They advertised it as, 'Sen-Sen. The original breath perfume.' You want one?"

Is he saying my breath smells? The aroma of licorice is so strong I can't control the urge to pinch my nose.

"I know," he says. "Kind of sickening."

What, me? My breath?

I don't want to breathe. My hair's stuck in my mouth, where it can stay. At least the wind diffuses the smell.

He's tall, but then everyone towers over me. If I could talk, I'd tell him, "Blow. Fly away home."

"Sometimes I wake up in the middle of the night and I can still taste licorice," he says. "Thank the Lord for Listerine." He makes the sign of the cross, then gurgles at the sky.

I wish he'd shut up. Where's Dad? What time is it?

"Sorry. I'm not being irreverent. Well, maybe a little." He cracks a grin.

He must be a total loser if he's talking to me. He is semi-attractive, in a nerdy way. Not that I'm judging him or dissing him. He's a boy. They're all alike.

Don't look at him. Don't listen. Don't even *think* he might be different.

All I can do is wait. Wait for my parents to rescue me, which they never do. I wish I wore a watch so I could stare at it, drop a hint. I've earned this window of trust with Mom and Dad and I'm going to need it. No cars in sight. No other place to sit. I can't just stand here like a target waiting for him, for someone, to attack me. I make a decision—return to the bench.

"The anemometer measured gusts of more than sixty miles per hour overnight." He slides in beside me, not real close. "Did I mention I'm addicted to the Weather Channel?"

I take out *Desire in the Mist*.

21

"There's weather on the Web too. Anywhere on earth, you can find out the weather."

Fascinating.

"You have hair in your . . ." He indicates his face and mouth.

With the corner of the book, I scrape the hair out of my mouth.

"I love a chinook," he says. "Except it's hard to talk over wind." He raises his voice a little. "Which is probably why I missed what you said." I feel his eyes boring into my ear. He sighs loudly. "How did you break your neck? Or sprain it?"

Page 143. Maggie Louise heaved a guttural sigh, her ample breasts expanding—

"The cast, or whatever that is, looks uncomfortable. Did someone drop you on your head?"

I squinch my ears shut before continuing to read . . . *ample breasts expanding in her Victoria's Secret—*

"Wait, don't tell me. Olympic tryouts. You look athletic."

I can't help cutting him a sideways glance.

"Aha! You landed a Rudi wrong. I've done that. Or was it a back salto with a double twist?"

I spin away from him again and hunch over my book . . . *low cut, lacy red corset that Charles had given her for Valentine's Day.* No one ever gave me anything for Valentine's Day. Well, Dad, but that doesn't count. I've never had a boyfriend and I never will.

The smell of licorice is overpowering and I shut down my senses to read. *Charles swiped his eyes with a knuckle. He said, "What about—"*

"A triple twist?" Green Boy interrupts. "A quad?"

Stop! Stop it. *"Forget Emilio," Maggie Louise sobbed. "There's only us. Only now." Maggie Louise regretted the words as soon as they left her mouth. She could never give up Emilio.* I turn the page. I wait for Green Boy to pipe up again, but he doesn't. Maybe he finally got the message.

She pressed her head to Charles's chest and felt her heart beat with his. Emilio. Oh, my love, Emilio. How could she tell him it was over?

Green Boy says, "I could show you my Rudi."

A drop of rain splats on my page at the exact moment Dad drives up.

"It's a rooty-tooty Rudi," Green Boy calls at my back. As I swing open the car door, I hear him mutter under his breath, "A rooty-tooty Rudi? God, tell me I didn't say that."

Over the racket of grinding up a steak and slimy gravy for my dinner, Dad shouts, "I'm really sorry I forgot."

Did you ever drink meat?

He apologizes all through the meal for spacing my schedule. "There was a fender bender and the interstate was at a standstill. It took me twenty minutes to get to an off-ramp. I'm so sorry, Daelyn. Thank you for your patience."

He says the words, but they don't ring true.

"I hope you didn't panic."

He hates it even more than Mom when I have a wack attack. One time we got on an elevator—I think we were going to the shrink—and it was around lunchtime and people kept rushing in, punching the Open Door button and crushing me against the wall where I felt trapped and couldn't breathe. I started to panic and hyperventilate, whimper and squirm because I couldn't get out, *get me out*, and Mom was there, telling Dad to punch the button for the next floor. He made people move and they got angry, then he yanked my arm too hard to pull me through the crowd because my feet were planted, they were glued to the floor, the faces of everyone scowling at me and Dad shouting, "Move aside! Let us THROUGH!"

His guilt trip for forgetting me at school gets me out of kitchen cleanup, at least. I go to my room and log on to Through-the-Light.

WTG is Ways to Go. How to do it. Methods and Means. Each is rated 1 to 5, low to high, in terms of effectiveness, availability, and pain.

Exsanguination (bleeding to death)

Effectiveness: 4–5, if you cut an artery. Otherwise 1–2.

Oh, now you tell me, I think.

Time: Minutes to hours.

Availability: 5. Razor-sharp knives are best. Razor blades are difficult to hold when they're covered with blood.

No kidding. I'd hated the blood. So much blood.

Pain: 2–3. Hurts at first.

Not that much. It hurts worse later, after you find out you failed.

Notes: Slitting wrists is a common suicide "gesture" and hardly ever results in anything more than a scar. Average time to die from a wrist-slitting depends on your height, weight, and how large and deep your wounds are. Expect at least two to four hours; longer if you weigh more or have increased body mass.

That was one miscalculation I made. Four hours, though? Of bleeding to death?

Strength and determination are required to cut deeply into groin or carotid arteries, which are the only wounds likely to kill you. Cutting your throat is difficult due to the fact that carotid arteries are protected by your windpipe. If you want to cut your wrists, cut along the blue vein on the underside of your arm. A hot bath helps, since it keeps the blood flowing quickly and slows down clotting. Position yourself so your wrists don't fall inward against your body, blocking off blood flow.

That was my second mistake.

Wouldn't the bath get cold in four hours?

Discovery danger is high.

Especially if you haven't given yourself enough time.

This is giving me anxiety, and I don't want to feel. I touch *FF* and scan the discussion topics. Same as before. I pick *Bequests*.

I leave my extensive LEGOS collection to Dmitri R*. I'd like Dmitri R* to take my dog.

J_Doe090859 should talk to Dmitri R* first. What if Dmitri R* doesn't want his dog? I'm pretty sure J_Doe090859 is a guy. Girls don't leave LEGOS as legacies.

I bequest and bequeeth my wedding vail to my beloved husband, Ferdnor, who proceded me in death. He passed suddunly last year from a massiave heart attack. I find I can not live without him. Nor do I want to.

So far on my list of property to bequeath I have my clothes, which should just be burned because Mom picked most of them out and they're hideous; my new computer, which isn't really mine because nothing Dad buys really belongs to me; my books, which I'm dealing with in my own way; and all my other earthly possessions that I threw into the closet when we moved here. If I were a generous person, I'd donate my stuff to a children's charity or something.

I'm not, obviously.

For trash day I'm going to gather a pile of old games and clothes and worthless junk that would only remind them of me, and shove them into a Glad bag. The next-door neighbors have tons of trash, so one more bag won't be noticed in the pickup. The trick is sneaking the bag out there without Mom or Dad seeing me.

Twenty-one more days to remove every trace of my existence. I could do that in twenty-one minutes.

- 20 DAYS -

No one calls me fat ass or lard butt at this school. No one smashes a Twinkie through my locker vent. No one pokes me and goes, "Gooey mass," or "Porker," or "Blubber belly."

Back in second grade this boy called me "Plumpkin." "Hey, Plumpkin," he said. "Hey, fatso."

I wasn't that fat yet. Maybe I was. I remember every mean thing anyone ever said to me. Plumpkin. Fat ass. Crybaby. Big fat crybaby.

It's so Oprah, but to feel better I ate away the pain. Then the pain ate me.

I don't know why I can't let the insults go, but I can't. I'm the product of every hurt that's ever been laid on me.

Human waste product. Dispose of it.

He's not there when I exit the gate. Thank God. I stalled around in the girls' restroom an extra few minutes so he'd give up.

Why isn't he in school, anyway? Even yesterday, when I got out early, he was there. He *is* a stalker.

It's a relief he's not here. I need to be alone, physically

and emotionally. The final act must be accomplished in a total state of purity. The other times, I realize now, I had impure thoughts. Doubt, or hope.

I open my book. The words glow stark against the page. Black, white, black, white . . .

"Sen-Sen?" he says, opening the tin.

I'd scream if I could. I'd tell him to . . . the word "respect" burbles up in my brain. Respect my space, my privacy. I don't deserve respect. I don't deserve anything. Mom's CR-V swerves around the corner and disorients me. How long was he there? Was I reading? Not one word sank in.

I hustle to the street and he calls, "Hey, you forgot your bookmark." I wrench open the car door and slam it shut. I have other bookmarks.

Mom says, "Hi, honey. How was your day? I missed you."

She never says that. Why would she miss me?

I almost look at her, then don't.

There are 318 people logged on to Through-the-Light. Friday nights are lonely for so many people in the world.

Not only have I never had a boyfriend, I've never had a date, so being home on Friday night is all I know. Mom and Dad used to have a standing Friday night date. Before, when they could leave me alone in the house at night.

The Final Forum is a beehive of activity. Buzz buzz. Hot topic tonight: *Attempts.*

J_Doe122589: How many times have you tried? This will be my third. And last.

J_Doe050550: I OD'd on heroin twice. My roommate found

me both times. He shoulda let me die, man. I'm so f*d up.

I could tell them stories.

J_Doe081967: I've tried 12 times. Pills, booze, knives. This time it's for real.

What a liar. Trying is failing. Failing to complete. Failing to plan and consider every angle of your method. There is always—ALWAYS—the possibility of failure. But twelve times?

I bet most of us here have tried and failed. The completers aren't here, of course. We're cowards in their eyes—if they can see us.

J_Doe102259 writes: *I try electric myself and didnt work. My frien told me if I drop hairdry in bath tub, I die. Wrong.*

Is she foreign or something? It's a global epidemic.

J_Doe012964 writes: *I chose electrocution becuz I read its fast and painless. I cut my electrical line and stood in bare feet in a puddle. I lost conshiousness and my neighbor resussitated (sp) me. All I got was 3rd degree burns on my leg. Its NOT painless.*

You never want to be resuscitated. You have to plan the time and place. You have to be alone. You never want to end up on life support, or as a vegetable. You must destroy your body beyond the point where it will support life.

The foreign girl adds: *I try total 4 times and evrytime I wake up in hopital.*

The worst is waking up in the hospital. Your parents are there, crying. Or your mother is yelling at the doctors and nurses. You come back wrecked. You ruin everyone's day.

It won't happen again.

I promise.

- 1 9 D A Y S , 1 8 D A Y S -

I wake with dread this Saturday. Not that I ever look forward to waking up, but weekends are especially bad. More time alone with them, their pathetic attempts to draw me out. "What should we do today, Daelyn? Go to an early movie?" Because I can't embarrass them in a dark theater, and the matinees are never crowded. "Play Monopoly? Or Clue? How about Pictionary?" When I don't answer, they give up. They've come to realize my only friends exist in cyberspace— like they're really friends. They're screen names. I don't do friends.

When I was nine, Mom said, "Would you like to be in Girl Scouts? I was a Girl Scout. You'll make a lot of friends."

By then being around a bunch of girls my age terrified me. "No thanks," I told her. Girls were so mean.

She said, "Go to one meeting. I bet you'll enjoy it."

No, no, no, no, no. She didn't get it.

She made me go.

At the meeting she stayed a few minutes, then left me at a stranger's house with all these girls who already knew each other. A few were in my class at school and one of them groaned. It clued in the others. The leader made the troop do a ceremonial welcome bridge and I had to walk under everyone's steepled hands. More than one girl tried to trip me.

The meeting was boring and stupid. One of the girls from my school came up to me afterward and said, "You'll like this part, Daelyn. It's where we eat." She gasped real loud so everyone would hear. "I hope we have enough cupcakes."

I went to the bathroom and locked myself in. The leader tried to talk me out, and even with my hands over my ears, I could hear the girls laughing at me. I sat on the floor against the door until Mom came to pick me up.

In the car she said, "Did you even try?"

Why do I have to be the one who tries?

In her eyes, I'm a failure. She won't miss me.

I'm required to keep my bedroom door open while I'm online, even though the first thing Dad did when we moved here was remove all the locks from the doors. I'm up before them so I log on.

Heavy topic on the Final Forum: *Sexual Assault*. I don't want to read those stories. *Bullied* attracts me again.

I was teased from kindergarten on because I'm gay. The teasing turned to bullying. J_Doe070790.

I've been called fag my whole life and I'm not even gay. J_Doe112985.

People call me pizza face. i can't help it if i have acne. They say "yo zit wad." girls back up when I come tward them. someone passed around a picture they drew in bio class. It was this sea monster tennacles. It had my name and unerneath they wrote ZIT SQUID. Everybody got a big kick out of that. i wonder how they'll feel when I'm dead.

J_Doe090291 writes: *Bullycide is the only cure for living.*

Bullycide. I know that word well. Suicide as an escape from bullying.

I touch the screen for *Add a Message*. A blank notepad appears with my ID filled in. My hands hover over the keys— five, ten seconds. I want to write my story. But if I do . . .

No.

I can't. I don't trust people anymore.

I go to touch screen off, but a new post catches my eye. J_Doe061890. *I was always the new girl, so people picked on me. I must've done something to deserve it otherwise why? I've been at this school for 2 1/2 years and every day these girls wait for me and hunt me down. They've threatened to cut me and beat me until I bleed to death. I'm going to save them the trouble.*

I key fast, "In first grade this boy said to me, 'You're fat. You're fatter than the fattest pig on the farm.' It made me cry. I told my mom and all she said was, 'Ignore it. Let it roll off your back.' How many times are you supposed to let it roll off your back?"

Just writing that much makes my pulse race.

J_Doe110282 writes: *The jocks call me queer fag sissy buttf*ck from the minute I get to school until I get out of there. I know it'll never end. Never.*

They kill you with their words. My fingers fly: "The first day in my new school these three older girls on the playground surrounded me. They were a pack. I was standing by the swings waiting for a turn and the leader said, 'You can't be serious. You couldn't even fit on that swing.' They all laughed. One of the other girls said, 'Even if you could squish in, we don't want you to break the new swing set.'"

J_Doe061890 replies: *"People are so f*ing mean. I hate everyone.* Join the biggest club in the world.

J_Doe100285 writes: *People teased me because of my disability. When I reported it nobody did anything. It just got worse.*

"I went to report them," I key, "but I found out the people with orange vests were the mediators. All three girls were wearing orange vests."

J_Doe061890: F* the entire human race.

Every recess. It was like they'd made a pact with every person at school. Don't let the fat girl play on any of the playground equipment. Don't play with her because she's fat.

Fat is ugly. Fat is stupid.

I cried every night. "I don't want to go to school," I told Mom and Dad. I begged them to let me stay home. Mom said, "You have to go to school. It's the law."

"Can't I be homeschooled?"

"We both have to work," Mom said.

They cared more about work than me.

I even told them how people called me names.

Dad said, "I got called names all the time because I didn't play sports. 'Wuss' and 'willy,' stuff like that. So what? Brains'll get you farther than brawn." He patted my shoulder. "Don't let them get to you."

But they are! I wanted to scream.

"Daelyn, what are you doing?" Mom walks into my room.

My fingers spring up off the keyboard. I raise my hand to cover the screen and it goes dark.

"Are you okay?"

I don't answer because I can't talk. Anyway, rhetorical question.

She says, "You look tired. Did you have a rough night?"

I don't sleep well. I have nightmares.

"I can't sleep either." She pulls her robe around her and hugs herself. "It was a hard week. I lost the account in Houston."

She doesn't sound sad, but I know she is. Losing work? Horrors. She pads over and squeezes me around the shoulders. I wince from the ache of her touch. I hate my skin for feeling.

Out of the corner of my eye, I see her looking around my room.

She zeroes in and crosses to my bed. Lifting my book off the pillow and flipping it over, she reads the blurb on back. A smile tugs her lips before she sets the book down. "They were difficult clients, anyway. Nothing I ever did was right. When your business is going under, you don't blame the accountant." She heads for the door and I think, No, you blame yourself. "You know what today is?" she says.

Mom smells good. She has this face cream that reminds me of peach pie. Don't breathe it in.

"The weekend. At last. Oh, don't forget we're seeing Dr. Novotny at one."

She pauses in the threshold. "You really do look tired, sweetheart. You should get to bed earlier. Get more sleep."

I intend to, Mom. Eternal rest.

* * *

Dr. Novotny is our fourth or fifth family therapist. I lose count. He says, "Hello, Daelyn." He wants to talk to me alone, I know. But I refuse. "Hello, Chip. Kim. Please, take a seat."

I want all of us, in unison, to pick up our chairs and leave. When Dr. Novotny runs out after us, Mom and Dad will say, "You told us to take them."

One, that would be amusing. Two, we are not amused.

"How is everyone?" He feigns interest. He has sweat stains under his pits. He looks like he doesn't get paid enough to spend wasted time with suicidal girls and their incompetent parents.

No worries, Dr. No. This is your final monthly torture session with the Rice family singers.

"Who wants to start?" he asks.

My hand shoots into the air and I wave it around going, "I do I do." Three—that wouldn't happen in this or any other life.

Dad says, "Daelyn seems to be doing well."

If only I could laugh, I'd give you that one, Dad.

"So the new medication is working?" Dr. Novotny peers intently at Dad. Like Dad would know. I'm supposed to let them in on how I'm feeling; if this antidepressant makes me sad or suicidal. What is beyond suicidal?

Dr. No turns to me, "How would you rate your happiness quotient, Daelyn?"

Oh, off the scale.

He probes my eyes, which is futile. I have nothing against Dr. No, personally, but he can't help me. No one can change the past.

35

Mom goes, "Daelyn seems much happier. She doesn't cry as much."

Because tears are useless.

Mom adds, "She's adjusted nicely to her new school. At least, that's my impression. Am I wrong?" She arches her eyebrows at me.

I don't look at her. I can't. I'm staring at Novotny's hair plugs.

He pushes a legal pad across the desk at me. There's a pen on top. I don't take them. What would I write? "Bald is beautiful"?

"She has a friend," Dad says.

I do?

"She does?" Mom and Dr. No say together.

"A boy," Dad explains. "I saw him talking to her on Wednesday."

"*That* boy?" Mom's voice takes on a sharp edge. "I told you not to talk to strangers, especially boys. He looks dangerous to me," Mom says to Dr. Novotny, to Dad. "Like a punk." To me she says, "He's not a friend of yours, is he?"

Does anyone see the humor in this?

Boys are *not* girls' friends. I've never known one boy who only wanted to be friends with a girl. Mom's right about them being dangerous.

She takes my limp hand and looks like she's going to break down. We're only five minutes into the session and already she's losing it. She doesn't usually disintegrate until we leave.

I hate to touch his filthy tablet. His nasty pen.

Mom holds my hand in her lap. "He's so . . . I don't know what you call it. Goth. Gangster." She says to Dad, "I don't want Daelyn associating with people like that."

He's so far from goth or gangster it's not even funny.

"He looks all right to me," Dad says. "Daelyn's going to have to talk to strangers sometime. I mean, everyone's a stranger at first."

For God's sake. I take back my hand and grab the tablet. In the bottom right-hand corner, in my tiniest print ever, I write: no.

I pass the tablet to Mom. She squints. Dad leans over to see. Even Dr. No is intrigued. I've totally made their day.

"No, he's not your friend?" Mom asks.

I know it's going to hurt, but I give Mom a definite shake of my head. The gesture rips my throat.

"Oh, Daelyn." Her eyes pool with tears.

I have to go. I have to go now.

Mom says at Sunday brunch, "Let's take a drive." Is it still brunch when your eggs and bacon are blenderized? When your waffles and strawberries are pureed and sipped through a straw?

I don't want to "take a drive." I want to go back to bed.

"We could drive up to Tiny Town. You used to love that place." She salts her scrambled eggs.

I never loved Tiny Town. It's this fake miniature town that some crazy person built. You walk around and peek into all the tiny windows. Then you get a sno-cone and come home.

"Is that place still there?" Dad asks. He separates the

newspaper, handing me the comics. I don't read the funny pages anymore.

Can I go to my room?

Mom reaches over and pats my wrist. "It'll be fun. Just the two of us."

I see her and Dad exchange a glance. Something's up.

I stand and leave the table.

Mom calls, "Take your jean jacket. It might get cool in the mountains." I close the bathroom door behind me. She'll hover between the kitchen and bathroom, timing me.

How to handle this? The jean jacket went in the trash on Thursday. It had a pink flowered frill around the bottom. So hideous.

I brush my teeth, not looking in the mirror. The sight of me sickens me. I flush the toilet and open the door so Mom doesn't die of asphyxiation from holding her breath.

As we head into the hills (I dressed in layers), Mom tells me about this time in high school when she tried out for pom-pom girls. What is pom-pom girls? It sounds obscene. "My friend Bonnie was the one who really wanted to make the team, and you had to try out in pairs. I'm not athletic, as you know, but we worked hard on our routine."

My mom's not athletic like the Pope's not Muslim.

She says, "I knew I was terrible, deep down, but Bonnie convinced me we'd make it. Deep down I knew she didn't mean 'we.' She meant her. *She* had to make it."

Did you know that deep down, Mom? Maybe you should mention it to Dr. No.

A wide-bed trailer stalls on the highway and Mom has to slam on the brakes. Instinctively her arm shoots out to brace me. I wish she'd swerved over the cliff.

We pass the trailer and Mom picks up where she left off. "The day of the tryouts I was so nervous. I think I actually threw up. Bonnie and I watched all the girls ahead of us, since we were last. They were good, but not as good as us, Bonnie said. She'd whispered in my ear, 'They're nowhere near as good as us, Kimmy.' Deep down I knew the truth. But she made me believe."

Deep down did you ever want to die?

"Her passion was contagious," Mom says.

This is weirdly similar to my audition, which I'd just as soon forget. The exit to Tiny Town is one more mile.

One more mile to sno-cone city.

"We got out there in our matching outfits that Bonnie's mother made, and the pom-poms we made. I don't even remember doing the routine. I didn't fall flat on my face." She smiles.

Is there a point to this?

"We had to wait for the results. It was nerve-racking. I thought for sure I was going to barf all over Bonnie." She gives a little laugh. Sort of hollow. "Suddenly I knew why I was doing this. For me. I wanted it. I wasn't the most popular girl in school, as you can imagine."

Why would I imagine that? I know nothing about my mom in school. Why wasn't she popular? Was she bullied? She wasn't fat, like me. She never talks about how it was for her growing up. She's never mentioned Bonnie, or any of her childhood friends. She signals to exit and slows for the turnoff.

"I lacked self-confidence. I don't know why. I was smart and people liked me. Being a pom-pom girl just seemed so out of reach for me. But I took a risk. I tried out."

This is more than she's ever shared, even in family therapy. I realize suddenly my mom and I are kind of alike. We have secret lives. The road to Tiny Town narrows and descends. "When the results were posted, I was stunned," she says. It grows dark as we veer into the forest.

I wait. She doesn't continue.

Come on, Mom. At least finish what you started.

"Ours was the only team," she says finally, "where one person got in and the other didn't."

I wish I could twist my head to look at Mom. In my peripheral vision, I see her eyes are on the road. She's smiling. Oh, my God. My mother was a pom-pom?

Her smile dissolves. "Bonnie made it."

I expel a short breath.

See? Life sucks. You have no power over anything.

We arrive at Tiny Town and Mom parks in the lot. She switches off the ignition and sits a moment. "I don't know why I told you that story." She shakes her head. "The things you remember."

Your failures and your faults. They stick with you. They glob into ugly, cancerous growths inside you and make you want to die.

The trip is a total waste because Tiny Town is closed until summer. The sno-cone stand is boarded up. Why do I think

Mom knew this the whole time? While we were away, Dad was busy at home. He installed a network to link his computer to mine.

He stands in front of the router, looking sheepish. "It shouldn't interfere with . . . whatever you're doing on your PC," he says.

What I'm doing can now be monitored 24/7. I'm not stupid.

Dad shrugs like, sorry. It was necessary.

"We love you," Mom says.

Can I go back to bed?

- 17 DAYS -

I count the minutes until school is out. I'm going through the motions, but it's draining. By the final bell, I'm sucked dry.

"On the weather wire, fair to partly cloudy with a twenty-percent chance of precip east of the Continental Divide. By morning, patchy fog with desire in the mist." He's reading from a little laptop.

I look at him for a minute and he says, "Cool, isn't it?" I'm guessing he means the laptop. He has this smirky smile on his face, like he's scheming, like he has me now.

He doesn't.

I swing my legs around on the bench, my back to him, and retrieve my book.

Maggie Louise felt his presence in the room. She dreaded this meeting with Emilio. She had to do it. For her. For Charles. The magnetism that drew her to Emilio was pure energy, bottled and fused. If you struck a match—

Heat prickles my skin, and it's quiet. He's stopped keying. I hear the lid click on his computer, and turn my head just a little. Because I don't trust him. What's he up to? I smell licorice on his breath.

"Okay. If geek gadgets don't impress you, how about this?" A hand stretches out over my shoulder with something furry clenched in it. "His name's Hervé."

I scream inside and lurch to my feet. It wrenches my neck.

"Hervé Villechaize."

Throat. Hurts. I need water.

The nose twitches and I drop my book as I'm tripping over a clump of grass to put distance between us. My mouth opens, but no sound comes out.

He gets up, adding, "Junior. We're in mourning because his brother, Harvey, passed on."

Oh, my God. What is that? Where'd it come from?

He holds the . . . the thing . . . to his lips and kisses it. Gross. "It'll be okay, Hervé. Harv's in a better place now. Pet him." He thrusts the thing at me.

I jump back. It's a rat. The hairless tail flicks around like a snake.

"When my winning personality fails me and tech toys don't tantalize, I find small furry rodents to be reliable chick magnets."

My eyes raise to his face. He's so weird. So . . .

His tender smile at the rat is kind of sweet.

"*Rattus norvegicus.*" The boy releases the rat onto his shoulder. The tail wraps around his neck and I wince, like there's a rope around mine. "Commonly known as the brown rat or fancy rat. Not because he's decked out in finery, but it seems some people fancy rats." He shoots that wide-open grin at me.

43

I focus on the rat, on filth. Rats *are* filth.

It's wearing a string harness, with a leash. Its front claws cling to the collar of the boy's crew. Both the rat and him are staring at me now. I feel it, the consensus.

I know I'm ugly. Don't look at me.

"You're not afraid of rats, are you?" he asks.

No, stupid. I'm terrified.

"Come on." He moves closer to me. "Pet him."

I rush back toward the gate.

"Wait. I'm sorry." He hustles by me, blocking my escape. "You didn't seem like the kind of girl who'd be squeamish."

He doesn't know what kind of girl I am. I'm not the kind who plays games and throws herself at boys.

He touches my forearm. "Come back."

I jerk away.

"Sorry," he says. He backs up a step, then two.

The bench or the hellhole that is school? What choice do I have?

He tracks me back to the bench, bending over to pick up my book. "In our last episode our heroine was tugging on our poor studly sap's heartstrings." He flips open to a random page. "Has she led him down the trail of broken tears?"

Just give it to me.

Seventeen more days.

The rat scrabbles down the boy's arm and sniffs the book. He chomps the cover.

"Hervé, no!" Boy wrestles book from Rat. "Sorry," he says to me again. "He's a voracious reader." A slick smile creases his lips as he hands the book to me.

44

Now it's infected with rat poison. I'm not touching it.

He studies my face for a long time. I KNOW I'm ugly.

He keeps looking. What? I'm not meeting your eyes. Uncontrollably, blood gushes to my cheeks.

He reads something in my face that's not there. "For us?" He cradles the book to his chest. "Hervé, the mystery girl has given us a gift. The gift that keeps on giving." He kisses the book and the rat rests a paw on it. "Hervé can really sink his teeth into fine literature like this."

I take out my pen and my econ folder. I write on the back page, "I hate rats. Fancy and otherwise."

He reads it. He mock spears a stake through his heart.

He's a dork.

He's confusing me because I think—I *know*—boys only want one thing. At least, in my experience. But he's not like any boy I've known. Maybe dorks are different because they can't get girls. Even with the dyed, spiky hair, and his cool demeanor, his swagger, deep down he's still a nerdy dork. Which makes him sort of desperate?

The laptop on the bench has a neon blue skin and I reach over to touch it. It is cool. Small and thin. I wish Dad had gotten me a laptop instead of a PC.

The boy sits and lifts the computer to his lap. He says, "You want to take it for a spin?" He opens the lid. "It's touch screen."

BFD. So's mine.

I shouldn't have violated his property.

I'm feeling my skin prickle again and he's smiling and the

45

rat is staring at me from the boy's neck and there's roaring in my ears and the gray is swooping in. One word flashes in my head: ESCAPE.

Where's Mom? Read, read. I have other books, but they're at home.

"There's no reason to fear rats," he said. "They have a language all their own, you know."

Mom's CR-V turns the corner and I leap to my feet.

He adds, "Like women."

I stumble to the curb and swing the door open. As I plop in, my labored breathing betrays me.

Mom says, "What's wrong?" Her eyes slit. "There's that boy again. Is he bothering you?"

I latch my seat belt. Go.

He approaches the car.

GO!

He knocks on my window. Mom says, "What should I do?"

I point ahead. My index finger jabs at the dash.

The window scrolls down. Is my mother insane? Don't talk to him.

"Hi," he says, leaning in. "I'm Santana. This is Hervé Villechaize Junior." He scratches the rat's head. Beady eyes burn me, Boy's and Rat's.

Mom looks freaked. I told you to go. You never listen.

"Okay, then." Boy backs up. "Hervé and I have a reading assignment." He winks at me and pats the book.

Mom looks at me too. What? What! I told you to go.

* * *

46

Carbon Monoxide Poisoning

Effectiveness: 4–5, as long as you're not rescued.

Time: Minutes to hours depending on concentration.

Availability: 5. Carbon Monoxide is emitted through car exhaust. To accumulate sufficient CO concentration (.32% to .45%), a confined area such as a closed garage is required.

Pain: 1, although symptoms are unpleasant.

Doesn't it stink? I wonder. Wouldn't you cough?

Notes: Actual cause of death is asphyxiation. CO binds to hemoglobin, crowding out oxygen, eventually leading to fatal hypoxemia. Early symptoms are headache, dizziness, and weakness, followed by decreased visual acuity, tinnitus, nausea, progressive depression, confusion, and collapse. Unconsciousness may be accompanied by convulsions. At .32% concentration, death occurs in approximately one hour. If you live, you will have brain damage.

Okay, that isn't an option.

What else?

Jumping Off a Building

Effectiveness: 4–5 for six stories or higher.

Time: Seconds (or hours if unlucky).

Availability: 4–5. You must have access to the top floor windows or roof.

Pain: 5. But if the fall is fatal, pain is over quickly.

Notes: Very frightening. Difficult to overcome fear of heights. Easily discovered if seen. Unsuccessful attempt is likely to result in paralysis or the possibility of spending your life confined to a wheelchair.

That is NOT an option.

This condo complex is only two floors anyway. The tower

at St. Mary's might be six or seven stories, but I'm not doing it there.

I hear a sound down the hall and freeze. It's Dad in his office. Is he spying on me? I power down, imagining the possibility that he might've seen what I read. My heart pounds like a jackhammer in my chest.

A person has no privacy anywhere. Ever since the first time I slit my wrists, I feel like I'm always being watched. If I'm not *looked* at or *sneered* at or *judged*.

Anyway, I'm going to die at home. That I know for sure. I don't want my body to be lost or mutilated so badly I can't be identified. My parents are annoying, but they shouldn't have to spend the rest of their lives wondering—or hoping—I'll return.

They are my parents, after all. My legacy to them will be peace of mind.

- 16 DAYS -

There's chorus rehearsal before school at 7:30 a.m. I'd circled it on Mom's schedule of events. The visual emptiness of my life, as it draws to a close.

"I don't get why you signed up for choral performance," she says as she backs out of the carport and into the street. "I wish you could explain that to me. There are so many other clubs and activities. Are you trying to draw attention to your—" She stops.

Failure? Abnormality? No, Mom. You do that for me by making me go to doctor after doctor and school after school.

It's just a joke, okay? Call it a tribute to Dad.

I keep my eyes on the road. Eyes on the road, Mom.

She gulps a breath, like she's losing it. God, don't cry. You see what good that does.

I'm sorry you don't get it, Mom. Sometimes I don't get why I do the things I do. I just know I wake up every morning and wish I was dead.

In chorus, standing there pretending to belong is part of my punishment. The other girls stare at me. I hear what they call me—the weird girl. The freak. They don't even bother to wait until I'm out of earshot to tell Mr. Hyatt they think it's ridiculous to let a mute girl sing in chorus.

They're right. But I want them—I want everyone—to see what they've reduced me to. A sick joke.

"She doesn't even mouth the words," JenniferJessica says. She's that mean girl from the restroom. Mr. Hyatt mumbles something about electives. Acceptance of everyone.

JenniferJessica goes, "Couldn't you at least put her in the back row?"

I'd laugh at that if I could. I'm short, so I have to stand in front. Factoid, JenniferJessica. It's not about you.

We're singing Bach's Minuet in G, which Mr. Hyatt arranged himself for our May Day concert. It's one of my favorite songs. I close my ears and block it out.

He's there, sitting on the bench, in my spot.

Waiting for me.

I know what it means when they wait for you.

Sixteen days, then the waiting is over.

I could stand inside the gate and hope he leaves. Or go back to the restroom. I hate the girls' restroom. I hate every second in school.

Irritated with myself, with my weakness, I push on the gate. He twists his head and smiles. "The beautiful mystery girl returns."

What a line. If he thinks I don't know what he's doing, he's dumber than I thought. I take out my notebook and write on the back cover, "Get off my bench."

He says, "Excuse me?"

I shove the notebook in his face. He grabs it and my pen. He writes, "I'll have you know this is *my* bench. I saw it first."

I take back the notebook. He's so juvenile. I don't know what to say, or do. I give him my dead zone gaze.

He says, "But I'm willing to share." He scoots over. Not far enough.

His teasing eyes hold no allure. Except now my stomach feels all fluttery. STOP. I stand a minute, sort of unsteady. Then my knees fail me. My skin, bones, nerves. Betrayal. For a fleeting instant, I wish I was still fat. I'd slam down on the bench and the repercussion would send him soaring.

Maybe he'd land on his thick head.

"Hervé wanted to come, but he's grieving. He's having a hard time getting over the death of his brother. Have a seat." He sweeps his hand above the bench corner, over my spot.

I swallow and it hurts my throat. The operation to repair my esophagus was a nightmare. I wish I didn't have to wear the brace, but I need it, especially now, to remind me of my mission.

"It was a natural death. Old age. Hervé's actually beating the odds." He's inched away from my corner while talking.

Thank you.

"Which gives me hope," he adds.

Whatever that means.

Despite my instincts and my better judgment, my determination and iron will, I lower myself to perch on the bench. He reaches into his back pocket and pulls out my book. Handing it to me, he says, "An enjoyable read. I want to know what happens in the first two hundred pages, though. Why are you tearing them out?"

I don't take the book, and I don't answer.

"All right," he goes. "I won't ruin the ending for you except to say Maggie Louise makes her choice. With an excessive amount of bosom heaving, of course."

The book is ruined now. He touched it. No telling where his hands have been. I've read it twice before anyway.

"She doesn't exactly redeem herself at the end," he adds. "I mean, she doesn't even apologize to Charles."

Why should she? I think. Charles deserves everything he gets.

I write in my notebook on a blank page, "There IS no redemption." I hold it up for him to read.

"For her?" he says. "Or him?"

I pull down the notebook and write, "For any of us."

He frowns. "You think?"

I write, "Therefore, I am."

He laughs. He has a rumbling laugh, like thunder.

Now I'm mad at myself for engaging him. He'll think I like him, and I *don't*.

He scoots closer and I edge away. He stops, scoots back, and sets my book between us on the bench. I reach into my book bag, which I'm keeping on my lap just in case I need to make a sudden and welcome departure. I pull out *Desire on the Moor*.

His head swoops down and around on his giraffe-like neck to check out the title. "Ah," he says. "The saga continues."

I open the book and start to read chapter one. He slides

all the way over to the opposite end of the bench and falls off.

I almost smile, then catch myself. *Chapter one. Magnolia Louise Delacroix awoke with a start. Would she find her Camelot today?*

Behind me, he goes, "Beautiful mystery girl on the bench, reading."

He's shallow if he believes I'll buy that line, or any line, or that I'm reading these books because I resemble Maggie Louise in any way. Maggie Louise is the one who's beautiful and mysterious. She's powerful and strong. *She always felt her Camelot was Charles, but lately he'd been preoccupied. And not with her.*

Boy sighs. Coming around the bench, he drops to the grass in front of me, rests an arm across one bent knee and says, "Since you asked, no, I don't go to school. I've been home-schooled all my life. I graduated early. Now I'm taking some time off, doing a pre-law course online. Everything you need to know can be accessed, digested, downloaded, podcast, and open sourced. Do you Wiki?"

When you Wiki suicide methods, your parents find out. They search your Google history and shut you down. Right now they could be tracing my access to Through-the-Light. I'm worried.

Homeschooled. How lucky. I wonder if it was his choice or his parents'. He's a combination nerd, geek, and dork. Plus, his ears stick out. Was he teased mercilessly and his parents were more sensitive, more sympathetic than mine?

He goes, "I hacked into the national weather service, but if you really want a mind freak, check out the patents at the U.S. Patent Office. I'll send you the link, if you have a computer."

I force myself to read.

"Do you? I pretty much spend all my time online."

That makes me glance up. He's a cyber mole, like me.

He leans back on both elbows and extends his legs. "Do you know there are 4,014 patents for different types of toilets? My favorite is the unisex activewear garment with fly flap."

Fly flap?

"That's right. Fly flap."

Stop reading my mind.

There's something about his voice I can't block out. His long, lean legs. I pinch my own nerve endings to numb all sensation and read, *Fog rolling in off the moor sent a chill up Maggie Louise's spine. She closed the shutters and scurried back to bed. Charles stirred, then rolled over and drew her into his arms.*

"Maybe we could IM."

I shrivel inside like a raisin. I'll never IM *anyone* again.

"My screen name is—"

Mom's here. I pack my bag.

"Wait." He scrabbles to stand and chases me to the curb.

I fling open the door.

He catches the strap on my book bag and I yank on it. But he only lifts the flap in front and inserts my book. My fouled *Desire in the Mist.*

His arm nearly decapitates me as he extends it through the window, across my face, and close to Mom. "We haven't formally met. I'm Santana Girard. The Second."

Mom has no choice but to shake his hand. The hair on his arm tickles my nose, and heat rises up my neck.

"I'm . . . Mrs. Rice. Daelyn's mother."

I bite my tongue. Bleed. BLEED.

"A pleasure to meet you." He retracts his arm. Then smiles at me.

He has a nice smile. No, he doesn't. And now he knows my name.

"Your daughter is a woman of few words."

Mom betrays me again. "She can't speak. She's—"

I press the automatic window to SHUT. HER. UP.

We drive away. I see the smug look on his face through the side-view mirror. He's jerking me around. Boys are jerks. Sex fiends. Why would I think he'd be different? If he thinks I don't know what he's doing by talking me up, lying about how beautiful and mysterious I am—

"He seems nice." Mom slows at the corner. "I prejudged him by his looks. That white hair, I guess." She pauses. "You don't need my approval to choose your friends. You know that, right?"

Breaking news, Mom. I don't choose friends. Which works out great because they don't choose me.

- 15 DAYS -

Friends is not a topic on the Final Forum. No one's here to make friends. In fourth grade this girl in school invited me to her birthday party and I was so excited because I'd never been to a birthday party. I got her a gift and wrapped it myself. Mom bought me a new dress. When we got there, no one was home. "Are you sure this is the house?" Mom asked. I showed her the address the girl had printed on a sheet of notebook paper. "Are you sure the party's today?" Saturday, the girl said. This Saturday at one o'clock. Across the street I saw a curtain move, then a face, two faces in the upstairs window. Behind the window a bunch of girls were pointing and laughing at me. I said to Mom, "I made a mistake. Let's go." She said, "Maybe I could find her number and call."

"Just go!" I cried.

The closest I came to having a real friend was this one time in middle school. She was new, this girl, and so was I. I never learned her name. I'd know her face if I saw her again, and I still hear her voice. She plunked down at my lunch table, said hi, and just started talking and eating a cold, fried, white cheese sandwich and checking out all the cute guys, and I was stunned and shocked because no one, not one person ever sat with me or talked to me at lunch, and finally she said in this strange accent, "Wat wid you? Why you look like dat?"

She meant dumbfounded. Or ugly. I couldn't speak. I mean, I could've, back then. I had functional vocal cords.

She shrugged.

She ate her whole lunch there, gabbing away at me, not even caring that I was this close to tears for sharing her company.

Kim and Chip are "having words." I hear them through the thin wall separating the bathroom and kitchen. I decided overnight it was time to begin detachment procedures. First step, refer to your parents by their first names.

Kim raises her voice. "How do you know she . . . ?" Her voice muffles and Chip garbles, ". . . saw the account . . ."

Are they talking about the computer? Damn. DAMN. They have no right to invade my privacy.

I sit on the side of the tub with my ear pressed to the wall. "Why didn't you tell me?" Kim snaps.

"I knew it'd upset you," Chip says.

"Of *course* I'm upset. I don't want collection agencies showing up at our door."

I lean away breathing a sigh of relief. They're only fighting about money—again. Why did they buy me this new computer? The old one was fine. They don't have to pay for a therapist or send me to private school, where I'm even more different from everyone else because I'm not rich. Rich girls are even meaner than regular ones, I'm finding out.

My eyes sweep the bathroom. Claustrophobic. Smaller than the last one, the third or fourth condo we lived in. We move a lot. Kim thinks changing schools is the answer to my suicidal urges. News, Kim. It only makes them stronger.

This bathtub is standard size. I guess they all are. I wish I'd known about a hot bath hurrying the process along. I didn't cut deep enough and I stalled too long mustering the courage. Then Kim came home.

Timing is everything. And method. When and how.

This bathroom, this toilet and tub, are basically mine, since Kim and Chip have the upstairs master suite. Kim bought me a battery-powered shaver, which is worthless on my leg and underarm hair. I can't have razors or electric appliances in the bathroom.

She even put a safety plug on the outlet. Kim, I want to tell her. Overkill.

The argument's over. They're sitting there, all quiet, when I trudge into the kitchen.

"Morning, honey." Kim forces a smile.

Chip says, "What can I get my girl for breakfast?" He pulls out my chair as he stands and passes behind me. His hand on my shoulder makes me wince.

He doesn't seem to sense it.

Smoothing the pleated skirt under my butt, I lower to the seat. Even though I've lost weight, I still feel squished and bulbous. I fold my hands in my lap.

Chip sets a glass of water at my place with two pills. I sigh inwardly. He and Kim watch and wait.

Today I'll take the pink pill first. My throat closes in anticipation. It still hurts to swallow them whole. Chip wanted to crush them for me, but the doctor told him they were time-release tablets, less effective if cut or crushed.

It goes down like gravel.

The white pill is my antidepressant. I hate to tell Chip and Kim no antidepressant in the world is going to change the past. I know medication is supposed to make me feel more hopeful and happy. What I need are performance enhancing drugs. Yeah, steroids. To make me powerful and strong.

Chip says, "So. Breakfast. Oatmeal or oatmeal?"

He's a real comedian.

Kim cracks a smile, though. She still loves him, I think. I haven't ruined that—yet.

A bowl of diluted oatmeal appears in front of me. It makes me want to heave. I can't eat another bowl of oatmeal. I never liked it before—

"Aren't you eating?" Kim says.

I try not to gag in her face.

"Don't you feel well?" She reaches over to palm my forehead. I try not to flinch at her touch.

She stares at me. Into me, as far as she can get. "Don't tell me you've stopped eating!" Her voice goes shrill. "You're not becoming anorexic, are you?"

Chill, Mom. I mean, Kim. Starving myself to death is way too slow.

Chip presses forward on his elbows. "You have to eat."

Or what? I'll die?

Okay. I sigh. One more bowl of oatmeal won't kill me. Unfortunately.

As I'm retrieving my book bag from the rocking chair in my bedroom, I take a quick inventory. There are six books left in the bookcase. I've spread them around to fool Kim. No problem reading six books in two weeks. These books are the only thing keeping me sane. Two piles of trash in the closet for two weekly trash pickups, which, hopefully, Kim won't mistake for laundry.

The computer. Fake posters on the wall. My rocking chair. I've had this chair since I was a baby. It's not really mine; it's Kim's. She rocked me to sleep singing Minuet in G. "How gentle is the rain . . ."

My throat catches. Kim, you can have the chair back.

She must've loved me once. My dad too. Everybody loves a chubby baby, right? Then you become a fat, ugly child who everybody bullies.

I have a test in econ today. Since my school days are numbered, I've renounced the act of studying. It's not like my GPA is crucial. Numbers are crucial. Everything is numbered. Fifteen days. The last bell, the twelfth bell of the day. When it rings, I count my steps to the exit. Thirty-three steps exactly.

He's there. What is his damage? Doesn't he have friends? Why doesn't he go IM his friends?

He's wearing a light-blue sleeveless sports jersey with the number 77.

"Ah," he says, "the beautiful mystery girl returns. She sits on the bench, daintily."

That's almost funny, since I just plopped down.

He hands me a wedge of paper, folded into a triangle. Actually, he sets it on the bench between us. He motions to it.

I want to, but . . .

I retrieve *Desire on the Moor*.

With his fingertips, he inches the note toward me.

I'm not watching.

Another inch.

Snatching up the note, I unfold it.

"I'm sorry," he's printed in green pen. "I didn't know you couldn't talk. I just figured you had amazing self-control." A down arrow.

I flip to the back, "You'd have to, to spurn my advances." I knew it! Sex is the only thing boys want. He says out loud, "I learned that expression from Emilio."

I lift my bag and take out my pen. I write on his paper, "Emilio does not speak English." I want to add, Jerk. I pass the note to him.

He reads it and goes, "Duh. I'm fluent in Portuguese."

Really? Do my eyes widen? He's lying.

He holds up an index finger. Whipping out a notepad he brought with him, he clicks a pen and starts scratching away.

I don't want to appear interested. I force myself to read from my book: *Maggie Louise felt Charles's manhood rise to the occasion. She smiled inwardly at her power over him.*

If only I knew where Maggie Louise got her power, her confidence. The only power I have over people is to leave them behind. And spurn advances.

He rips out the page and sets it on the bench.

I pay no attention.

End of page 32. I tear the page out of the book.

Page 33. . . . marveled at the outline of Charles's muscled arms and back. "Are you sure you don't want to go on the fox hunt today?" he asked.

Boy taps the paper.

"Quite," she said. They'd only been at Longshead two days and already she was speaking like a proper Brit. "I thought I might go into Wiltshire for a bit."

"A bit of what?" Charles asked. Maggie Louise laughed. Charles wasn't laughing. What was that tone in his voice?

Boy slaps the note against the page I'm reading and jostles my book. He'd printed in block letters, YOU'RE ONLY MAKING ME MORE DETERMINED.

That's your problem, I think. I refuse to touch anything he's touched, so I shake the note off my book.

He sighs. "Did you get the message Hervé left in your book?"

What message? I keep my eyes on the page. Now I've lost my place.

"He has the hots for you."

I hate that expression. How many times have I heard, "Blah blah has the hots for you," when people are making fun of me? No one has the "hots" for me or ever will. Not even a rat.

Ever since Emilio . . . I skip to the last paragraph. *Ever since . . . No. She and Charles had moved beyond the affair. Charles had said, "We'll never speak of it again." Even though Maggie Louise had promised, vowed, pledged her heart and soul to Charles, a sliver of doubt . . . No. She wouldn't allow herself—*

62

He's written a new note and he slides it over my page. Quit it! My eyes flicker across and down.

HOW DO YOU SPELL YOUR NAME? CHECK ONE:

____DALEN

____DAYLYN

____DA-LN

____DATELINE

____DARELING, DAKON, DEFCON, DOWNTOWN, DOWNWIND, AM I GETTING CLOSE?

I wish I had a memory zapper so I could make him forget my name. Before I can remove the note, he takes it back and writes more.

FILL IN THE BLANK. HI, I'M THE BEAUTIFUL MYSTERY GIRL ON THE BENCH. SITTING DAINTILY. READING. MY NAME IS_____. WOULD YOU GO OUT WITH ME?

My face flares. He's baiting me. Am I asking *him* out? Get real.

A pen dangles in front of my face.

I use my own pen and fill in an X for my name. And no at the end.

"I knew that was too easy." Shifting, he sticks out his legs in front. He's wearing baggy camo shorts with the sleeveless football jersey. Those long, skinny legs. Stick-out ears. If he has muscles anywhere, I don't see them. I'm not looking.

He raises his arms and flexes his fingers over his head. "Okay, Daelyn, however you spell it. Here's the deal." He has fuzzy pits.

"The deal is this. If you want me to leave and never speak to you again, blink once."

I blink.

"If you're playing hard to get, blink once."

I blink. WAIT.

"If you've been rendered speechless by my incredible masculine physique, my charming wit, my magnetic personality," he flexes his fingers in front of him, "my wide array of interests and talents, my apparent intellect, charisma, and irresistible way with women . . . blink once."

I can't stop my blink.

"Aha!" He points. "I knew it."

He's insufferable. I learned that word from Maggie Louise.

Kim pulls up.

"Yo. Yo, mama." He shoots to his feet before me. He waves at her as he extends a hand to help me up. But I can't. His touch will contaminate me.

I drop my book into my bag and, rushing by him, scurry to the curb.

"Hello, Mrs. R," he says as he opens the door for me. He's beaten me to the car. "How was your day?"

He's in my way. Please, read my mind now. Go away.

Kim says, "Long."

"What sort of work do you do?" he asks.

Move. Okay?

She answers, "I'm an auditor."

"Oh wow. That sounds fascinating. I'm a numbers man myself."

Mom meets my eyes. The panic on my face must clue her in.

"Would you mind?" she says to him. "Daelyn has an appointment."

"Oh." He steps back, right into me. Clenching my arm to keep his balance and/or steady me, he says, "Sorry." My skin burns. He smells like hair gel and boy and this blue-white heat streaks through my body.

He steps away, and I feel a panic attack coming on. An object slips into my hand. The edges are pointy sharp, but instinctively my fingers curl around them.

"Nice talking to you, D." He waits to ease the car door shut behind me. Flicking a stiff thumb at Kim, he makes a clicking noise in his cheek and says, "Catch you later, calculator."

It makes Kim laugh.

"He's cute," she says as we drive off. "What's his name again?"

I take a deep breath, then crank up the radio to drown out the static.

I try to throw the note into the trash can, but it sticks to my clammy palm. I fling my book bag onto the rocking chair and shake the note off onto my desk.

If I open the note, it means I care. I can't care. Not now. I'm on this path, this mission. The only power I have in my life.

Perched on the edge of my bed, I stare at the note. Forget it. I move to the other side of the bed and gaze out the window. A guy is tossing a Frisbee to his dog who's leaping up to snag it. He motions to the dog, like, higher? The dog barks. Higher? He's teasing him.

I hate teasing. That dog should bite that man.

"Hey, Daelyn. You want my brownie?" This girl in elementary school taunted me. Mean girl. They're always mean. I got up to take the brownie and she threw it to her friend across the cafeteria. "Go get it, bloater. Fetch."

I almost did. I wanted that brownie. The only time I felt happy was when I was eating. Food was my BFF.

The dog retrieves the Frisbee.

I twist my torso to look at my desk. At my computer. The note beside it.

I close my eyes and black out the day. The exhaustion of living through it, surviving. Reaching up, I rip the Velcro tape on my neck brace to loosen it. From the front, I remove the hard plastic tube, then lie back on the bed, the brace dangling from my hand. It clunks on the floor.

The relief to be free of bondage is incredible. I should go without the brace and collapse my trachea again. Destroy it the way I did when I . . . failed.

Unfortunately I start to cough. Kim runs in. "Are you okay?" She must've been lurking outside the door.

I hold up a hand. Kim jerks me upright and the phlegm clears from my throat. She runs out for a glass of water.

I want to tell her, Please, Kim. Stop trying to save me. You couldn't then; you can't now.

When we first moved to this condo six months ago, and even before that while I was recuperating, I used to keep track of who came to check on me and when. I'd note the time. Dad, 9:15. Mom, 11:56. Dad, 4:32. Mom, 8:01. They never came together. Occasionally one of them would linger at the door.

During those times they'd stand there watching me watching them, I'd pray, Please. Put a pillow to my face. Clench a hand around my throat. Stab me. Shoot me. Put me out of everyone's misery.

Why did you give birth to such a loser? Why didn't you admit I was hopeless and fat and stop trying to make me fit in? This world wasn't meant for me. I was born too soon, or too late. Too defective.

I wish I could tell my parents, "If you want to help me, help me die."

I wonder, Are they required to fill out a 24-hour suicide watch form? Is The Defect at home? Check. Is It alive? Check.

Why did they bother with the corrective surgery on my throat anyway? Waste of money. They threw away, or hid from me, everything with sharp edges, or breakable. Picture frames. Pottery. Did they think they could suicide-proof this place?

I want to tell them, "Chip, Kim, there is no way to suicide-proof a person."

I key in the Final Forum, "My 2nd grade teacher told my parents I was hypersensitive. That I cried over nothing."

Nothing. You call it nothing when people make fun of you all the time? When you are always the target? You call it nothing when people *touch* you? My veins throb in my neck and I clench my jaw.

I key faster, "No one wanted to sit by me. They said I smelled. This kid plugged his nose every time he passed by me. He'd say real loud, 'P.U. Did you fart?' I wanted to fart in his face."

I pause over the keyboard. How stupid. I remember that like it's yesterday. All the mean things people did to me, said to me. They've built up.

What time is it? Late. It's pitch black in my room and silent.

Kim and Chip are sound asleep—I hope.

"A while later," I continue to key, "we came back from gym and my face was red from doing gymnastics. I was overweight. Needless to say, gym was not my best subject. Everyone sat down and there was this loud farting sound. People laughed and pointed at me. That boy had put a whoopee cushion on my seat."

Their laughter echoes in my ears, still. I have to cover them to mute the volume.

A minute later, I open my eyes and read what I've written. It seems trivial. Even funny, to some people. But back then, in second grade, it was like a defining moment in my life.

J_Doe111091 responded: *My teacher used to play pranks on me. Like he'd lock me in the art closet after school. Then he molested me.*

He, or she, should've put that in *Sexual Assault*.

I remember my teacher was laughing at me too about the whoopee cushion. Big joke. I felt myself shrinking and fading away. I wanted to eat. I wanted to die. All year long boys made farting sounds with their hands in their armpits. Girls called me THE BIG FAT FARTING PIG.

J_Doe092892 writes: *I quit school halfway through 8th grade. I couldn't take the shit. It was either kill everyone or kill myself.*

I couldn't quit. My parents wouldn't let me.

I'm still back there, dying inside.

* * *

If I prop up two pillows I can lie down in bed without my brace. I wish I had a laptop. My head can turn without too much trauma if I'm at a forty-five-degree angle. I see the wedge of paper. It can sit there for the rest of my life.

15 days. Occupy my mind. How many hours is that? I break down the equation in my head:

15 days X 24 hours in a day = ?

15 is the sum of 10 and 5.

10 X 24 = 240

5 X 20 = 100

5 X 4 = 20

240 + 100 + 20 = 360

360 is the circumference of a circle. I will have come full circle.

In how many minutes? 360 X 60 minutes. Too many to calculate in my head. More than a few. My focus wanes and my eyes flicker over it. I'm not opening the note.

Self-control. He got that right.

I gaze up at the ceiling. Through it. Past Kim and Chip's room on the second floor into the sky, space, heaven, hell. Who says hell is down? It could be up. It could be next door to heaven. Hell could be a subset of heaven, like a ghetto in the middle of a glass city.

How long will it take for me to get to where I'm going? It will be instantaneous, I hope. Do you actually walk through the light? Of course you don't walk, because you're no longer a physical presence. Do you feel it, though? Do you know you've passed to the other side? On TV you do.

I've never been afraid of the dark. I'm more afraid of the day, of people. I love the night. The solitude. Well, I don't love it. I don't feel love. I hate people, so I hope when I get there it isn't crowded. I hope the light is a momentary phenomenon and the other side is completely black.

And silent.

My throat feels like it's closing, so I roll over onto my side. Secret note from Hervé. I'm so sure.

It worries me that Chip might see what I write in the Final Forum. I didn't tell Chip or Kim what was happening at school. Not the later stuff, after the closet incident. I don't want to go there yet.

They had to hear my incessant plea: "I don't want to go to school. Please don't make me." Day after day.

Year after year. "Please don't make me go."

"You have to go," Kim would say. "It's a new school. Make a new start."

"Sticks and stones," from Chip. Words will only kill you.

I gave up pleading with them. I just gave up.

I return to the desk and delete my entries from the forum.

I'm not going to open that damn note. Or that closet door.

- 14 DAYS -

I don't sleep. All night long I'm wide awake, thinking, Secrets,
secrets, secrets. There are secrets in my past no one needs to
know. Secrets in my present that might kill Kim and Chip.
I don't want to take my secrets with me when I go. When I
pass through the light, I want to be free of everything and
everyone.

Through-the-Light.

I'm addicted.

Welcome, J_Doe071894. You have 14 days left. Will you be
prepared? Yes No

I touch *Yes.*

It's dim in my room; the sun isn't up. There's no stirring
overhead and no one's come to check on me for an hour. Maybe,
finally, they're trusting me to make it through the night.

The sad truth is, they should never trust me.

I need to know how secure I am online. In the menu I find
the privacy policy and read it all the way through.

Through-the-Light collects no personal information about its
members. Your activities, while monitored by system administrators,

are transparent to networks and central servers. Our patented Enigma encryption software completely cloaks access, usage, and online transactions. URL crawls to and from Through-the-Light are undetectable even for authorized users.

Really? It seems too good to be true. I don't trust it. I don't trust anyone.

Another line catches my eye. *Once you delete your account, you can never reenter Through-the-Light.*

One chance. No turning back.

My stomach churns. This is my final opportunity to get it right.

I check the DOD list. Only three names. Wait. It's populating as I watch. Four, five, six. People must live in different time zones or something. Eight, nine. Live and die.

Secrets. I can't take them with me. If I do, when I go, when I arrive at my final destination, I'll be . . . impure. I have no choice but to trust that they're safe here.

I touch *Final Forum.*

Bullied.

I key, "I wasn't the only fat kid in school. There were others. They got bullied too. This one kid, a fifth grader, brought a knife to school and had a wack attack, just yelling and threatening people. It happened on the playground at lunch. He got expelled. I heard rumors that he moved, then killed himself."

J_Doe050881 writes: *You try to take on the tormentors. But there are always more where they came from.*

Exactly. So your only other choice is to take out the tormented.

This other girl was a cutter, I remember. She was in my reading class. I could see the scabs on her arms. At ten, she was already cutting.

At ten, I was planning my death.

An alarm clock buzzes upstairs and I power down. The sun's up. A new day is beginning. Or ending, depending on where you are.

Already I'm exhausted. I rest my forehead on the desk, but it stretches the back of my neck and that hurts. I turn my head. There's the note.

Secret note from Hervé. He'd said, "Did you get it?" Before he forced this note on me.

I get up and retrieve my book bag from the rocking chair. I open the front pocket where he'd slipped *Desire in the Mist*. What did Hervé leave in it, a rat turd?

Inside the front cover, printed in blue ink, is one word: HERVEHOTSU.

What is that? Portuguese? Hervehotsu. Stupid. It's like a screen name.

A screen name. HerveHotsU.

I throw the book in the trash.

The shower goes on upstairs and footsteps creak in the hall. Watching. Always watching. I snatch the note and take it with me to the bathroom.

On the toilet, I dig out the flaps and unfold the wedge of note. In black pen, like calligraphy, elegant letters centered on the page:

IM me

The last time I got baited into IMing, people wrote nasty, hurtful messages.

I won't set myself up again.

I tear the note to bits and flush it.

School is school. I dreamwalk down the halls. I pass the time wishing I was gone. We get our tests back in econ and I got a D-. A red scrawl under the grade reads: *See me after class.*

For what? Confession? Why did Kim and Chip pick a Catholic school? I don't even believe in God.

My test is snatched off my desk. This girl sitting next to me covers my paper with her arm and does something. Writes on it. When the teacher isn't looking, she slides the test back onto my desk.

She'd extended the legs of the *D* to make it look like an *A*. *A*-.

She's smiling.

At me.

Why?

The bell rings and I'm the first one out the door. I hustle to the restroom. In a stall, I rip the test into shreds and cram them into the used tampons container.

Don't touch me.

He's there after school sitting on the bench with his arms resting across the back. My stomach flips. STOP.

Why? Why are people making contact NOW?

I retreat into the building, into the bowels of hell.

He needs to go. They all do. They need to know I'm not doing this with them.

- 13 DAYS -

Trash day. I keep a box of Glad bags behind the bottom drawer of my dresser. I hope Kim doesn't pull out the drawer. My clothes are sparse. I have underpants, socks, a bra. I've never owned much, since we move so often. I don't care about keeping stuff. I spread what little I have evenly between all four drawers. Behind the fourth drawer are my plastic bags.

Kim didn't even think about locking them away. Heads up, Kim.

Plastic bags are a suicide completer's best friend. Especially if you choose to overdose. Drug overdose is an unreliable method, I read, because height and weight, general health, gag reflex—all of these work against you. On Through-the-Light it's recommended that, in addition to taking as many pills as possible, you slide a plastic bag over your head and secure it with a belt. That way if the drugs don't do their job—if they take too long or you panic—suffocation will render you unconscious.

Even if I had access to my pills, I couldn't get enough of them down my damaged throat now.

Into a trash bag goes my slim stack of clothes and toys and the gilded jewelry box that Kim got me for my twelfth birthday. She asked, "Do you want to invite some friends over for cake and ice cream?" I said, "No." I thought, Please don't make me. The one time she listened. She said, "Okay, then. It'll just be the three of us."

The music box plays "A Time for Us." Ironic.

Maybe I won't throw it out yet.

The book is still in the trash can by the desk. How could I be so stupid? What if Kim found it and read the message? She wouldn't understand, but she'd spend a lifetime trying.

That could be her penance.

No, I'm not that cruel. I rip out the first page and bury it in the Glad bag.

We have chorus rehearsal today for the May Day concert. I won't be around for it, but I committed to chorus. I'm all about commitment.

JenniferJessica keeps pushing me, nudging me, pressing her shoulder against mine. I want to tell her to cool it. Then the other girl on the left side of me starts doing the same thing.

I move back and the girl behind me pushes me forward. They always come in packs of three.

Mr. Hyatt stops rehearsal. "What's going on?" he asks.

JenniferJessica says, "Nothing."

I say nothing, of course.

He purses his lips. The rehearsal resumes and so does the pushing. I want to scream, Stop it! Stop touching me. In this one middle school, people would shove me or push me in the hall. I wanted to chase them down and shove them so hard they fell on their faces. But then I'd get in trouble or they'd retaliate. In class, this one boy sat next to me and poked me in the arm. Just poked me. He'd press his finger into my skin until it made a dent. Why? Boys were always being pushed into me. They stuck notes on my back: KISS ME.

PIGGY BACK.

JenniferJessica pushes me out of line.

Mr. Hyatt motions for the pianist to cut. He says, "Daelyn, would you mind singing alto?"

Am I supposed to answer?

JenniferJessica snorts. Everyone around us snickers and the roar in my ears crescendos.

I shuffle over to the alto section. The joke's on you, bitches. I sing alto.

"You can stand by me," a voice says. It's the girl from econ. She has a face now. A face and a voice. Round face. Soft voice.

"We can share music."

I feel grateful. STOP. Don't feel.

He's not on my bench. I don't mean "my." Nothing belongs to me. I close the gate and walk past the tree. He doesn't leap out to ambush me.

You have no idea how relieved I am.

I sit and set my book bag next to me; pull out *Desire on the Moor*. Exhuming the weight of the day, my bones go Jell-O and my muscles melt. I read, *Maggie Louise took the outstretched hand that the Frenchman, Jean-Jacques, offered her. She was a deft horsewoman, but if a man—this man—wanted to help her dismount, she certainly wouldn't refuse the offer.*

Santana's plotting a sneak attack, I think. Waiting until I'm engaged in my book, then WHAM.

I'm so wise to sneak attacks. It won't happen to me again.

I just called him by his name.

Detach.

"Do you wish me to cool your mare down, Miss?" Jean-Jacques crooned in his sexy French accent. He took the reins from her, touching her fingers lightly with his gloved hand. She'd never known a stable boy to wear leather gloves. Soft, creamy kidskin. If the gloves hadn't given him away, his impeccable manners and grooming would have. "Who are you?" she asked. "Really."

He'd introduced himself as the trainer at Longshead, but Jean-Jacques was no stable boy.

I suppress a yawn. It hurts to yawn. Especially in the back of my throat where the stitched skin catches. He's late, if he's coming. I don't care if he's early or late. I don't want him springing out of nowhere is all. With a rat.

"For me to know. And you—"

"To find out," Maggie Louise finished.

No one ever found out what was happening inside me. How the pain was eating me away. No one ever came to my rescue, or stood up for me.

I smell licorice. It alerts me.

I'm at the ready as I read fast, *Jean-Jacques bowed. Maggie Louise caught the teasing glint in his eyes. The game was on.*

No movement around me. No presence. Phantom scent of licorice. It's my paranoia. I'll never lose it.

I wish I was Maggie Louise. Trusting, desirable, loved. Maggie Louise had lovers everywhere because she loved herself. Even if she wasn't the most admirable person—always cheating on Charles, expecting his forgiveness—Maggie Louise saw what she wanted and took it. She'd never allow people to treat her like dirt. Charles, on the other hand . . .

Who cares about him? He's weak and powerless in her hands.

I tear out the page.

A footstep sounds behind me and I brace. The jangle of keys. A thud. Turning my torso slightly, I spy the UPS man heading into the building. The truck idles right in front of me.

My vision blurs. Where was I? On the bench, with the book. In the body of someone I'll never be. I rip out this page and the next.

I'm only on page 59 and there are thirteen days left. Thirteen days to finish this book and the next, *Desire in the Mine*. I rip out a fistful of pages.

For a while I sit and stare into space. At the truck, a passing car. A slight longing seeps in and I can't will it away.

I wish I could drive. I'll never reach my sixteenth birthday.

Where would I go, anyway? To the mall with all my friends?

When Kim pulls up, I stand. *Desire on the Moor* flutters to the ground. I think to leave it, but I don't want *him* finding the book. Leaving me a message.

"Where's Santana?" Kim asks.

Like I know or care.

A total of thirteen people are on the DOD list tonight. I shouldn't think of them as people. What are they now? Spirits? Energy? They're happy; that's all I know. They're free.

It's Chip's turn to invade my privacy. At least he knocks first, which gives me time to power down. "What are you doing?" he asks.

I just look at him. He wanders over to my desk. Instinctively my hand raises to cover the monitor.

"What were you working on?" He hitches his chin at my PC. "Just now."

I should've thought to open textbooks on my desk or something. Think, think. I retrieve my book bag and take out a spiral. I find a pen.

I print, "I'm writing a story. For English."

Chip reads my note. "I saw you Google, then nothing."

I take back the spiral. I'm not sure what to say. Chip touches my shoulder and I flinch. When did I start to cringe at his touch? He goes, "Can I read your story when it's done?"

I print, "It's boring."

Chip chuckles. "I doubt that." He stays too long, checking his watch. "Well, I'll leave you to it."

After he's gone, I log back on. For Chip's sake, I Google "Shakespeare." I choose "Collected works." In another window I'm back at Through-the-Light.

I touch *WTG*.

Explosives

Effectiveness: 4–5 if detonator works properly.

Time: 10 milliseconds (approximately).

Availability: 1.

Pain: 4–5, but quick.

Notes: Difficult to acquire effective explosives and a detonator. Do NOT use gunpowder or other "slow" or homemade explosives. Use dynamite or "plastique." Strap it to your forehead with the detonator. Taping a grenade to your head will work as well.

Oh, right. Where would I get a grenade? Kim, next time you pass through airport security, could you see if anyone's confiscated a wad of plastique and a detonator?

I link back to DOD. Three more. It's comforting, somehow, to know I'm not alone.

Too bad I'll never see my name on this list. Unless you can access Through-the-Light from the afterworld. Not on a computer, of course. I wonder, though, if you're all-knowing, all-seeing. If you choose to, can you monitor activities here on Earth?

Not that I'd want to. But if your reasons for leaving are to spite someone, or to hurt someone, it might be useful.

Mine aren't. I just want the pain to end.

There are people who are leaving to get back at others, though. J_Doe111192 wrote on the Final Forum: *My bf broke up with me 8 months ago today. Every day it hurts more and more. People tell me time will ease the pain, but it's not. I found out he's engaged and his fiancé is pregnant. He got me pregnant and made me get an abortion. I'm only 17. He killed our baby and he killed me. I want him to feel dead inside the way he makes me feel every day of my life.*

How does she know he'll even care?

The Final Forum is teeming with people who hate

specific individuals. J_Doe122388 wrote how his three older brothers beat on him: *They'd call me worthless pig shit and kick and punch me. Two held my arms while the other burned me with a lighter. Our dad hit us too but it hurt worse when my brothers took it out on me.*

I'm glad I don't have siblings.

J_Doe060391: In 7th grade I had this bff who I trust with my life. I told her everything all my secrets what happened to me when I was little. See my mom had a drug problem and sometimes she let men take pictures of me. I showed one to my bff and the next day it was on MySpace and everyone's calling me a whore. She said she couldn't be friends with a child porn star. IT WASN'T MY FAULT. Why'd she do that? Why'd she tell?

Because no one can be trusted.

In one day I count fifteen stories where people are cyber-bullied. Like, they'd get texts or IMs harassing them, then telling them they should die. I guess they figured they might as well do it.

I've been there. People trick you by saying, "Let's IM," and you're so desperate to believe they're serious, you give out your screen name. Words pop up on your screen. "Oinker." "Jiggle jugs." Messages like, "Derek is hot for you. He wants to take you out on a date." You think, Really? Until the next IM: "At the all-u-can-eat buffet."

Why are people so cruel? What did I ever do to them?

I can't even count the number of stories in the Final Forum about gay people coming out. This one J_Doe wrote that his mother said, *I wish you'd never been born. You've ruined this family.*

That'll make you want to die.

Some kid's father told him, "I'd rather kill you than have you be gay."

He's saving his father the trouble.

Kim's never said anything like that to me—I'd rather kill you than have you be fat. But she never just accepted me for the way I was. She was always, "Let's try this new diet. We'll do it together. I could always lose ten pounds." She was thinking, And you could lose a hundred. Of course, I'd cheat. Or cry at the table. Then Chip would sneak me snacks at night. I don't blame him for sabotaging my diets; he had to be on them too. Hurting Kim or Chip is not my intent. I have no intent. I have no reason to live, that's all. When I'm gone, I don't *want* to be remembered.

I'm starting to feel anxious, so I log off. A tap on the door and Chip sticks his head in. "Whatcha doin' now?"

If you only knew, Chip.

He eyes me and the computer. "Working on your story still?"

I don't answer. He says, "Mind if I test something?"

He comes in and I get up out of the chair. I move to the bed. He powers on my PC and goes, "I sent you a message. I just want to make sure you got it."

Don't lie to me, Chip. All men are liars. I hate believing my dad is one of "those men."

It's hard to watch him sitting there, keying into my computer, hoping to key into my brain.

It's the one place you have no access to, Chip.

"Is it a Word file? I won't read it—unless you want me

to." He swivels his head and smiles. There's, like, terror in his eyes.

I can't look at him.

He turns back. "Everything seems to be working."

Except me. I'm broken.

"Okay. All your files are set to 'shared.' I promise not to read them unless you ask me to."

I wish I could trust him, my own dad. He's the one who hacked into my computer and found out I'd been on the suicide boards again. Strictly verboten.

I wonder how he'd react to Through-the-Light. If he believes a Web site has the power to influence me to kill myself. Would he find the comfort I do in knowing I'm not alone? In feeling acceptance for my decision? No one's putting thoughts in my head, Chip, that weren't already there.

He stands. "How about a bowl of Ben and Jerry's?"

That's his answer to everything. It used to be mine too. Now I have a more permanent solution.

I get up to follow him.

I can't sleep. I know what's bugging me. I need to choose a method. The last method I chose was absolutely wrong.

To sit at my desk, I have to strap on the neck brace. It's a pain.

I log on to Through-the-Light and select *WTG*.

Bullet to the Head

Effectiveness: 4–5 if done properly.

Time: If well aimed, instantaneous.

Availability: Easy in USA; more difficult in countries

where guns are illegal, such as UK, China, Australia.

Pain: 4–5.

Notes: If you don't die, you will experience excruciating pain and brain damage. Lots of willpower is needed to fire a gun at yourself. Bullet can miss vital parts in brain or deflect off skull. Preferable to use a shotgun rather than a pistol. For ammunition use .458 Winchester Magnum or soft-point slugs with .44 Magnum. People usually survive single .22 shots to the temple. Extremely messy for people who have to clean up after you.

No blood this time. Chip and Kim are still recovering from all the blood after the times I slit my wrists. Yeah, I failed more than once trying that method.

Someone's coming. I have to power down.

Lie in bed. Play dead.

It's Chip again. I know his breathing. I make sure he hears mine so he'll leave.

As I lie there, breathing audibly, I'm thinking, Stupid screen name, hervehotsu. Why'd he have to make it so memorable?

I haven't used IM in years. Not since the last time someone wrote, "r u the freak who slit her wrists? Why didnt u die?" That was long before Chip and Kim took my computer away the last time. When I got it back, it was understood: New start. Renewed trust. But we will restrict your usage with parental controls and traces, the way we did before. Please, Daelyn, promise. No suicide chat rooms.

I want to tell them, Kim, Chip. Computers don't kill.

I wait for his footsteps on the stairs.

All this up and down, bed to desk, is taking it out of me.

The weakness, the emotional and physical impotence makes me do it. I check my old screen name. It's there. How weird. People could be history, gone for years, and their IM accounts would still be active. If I'd known, I never would've laid tracks.

I create a new screen name. Random letters and numbers. It makes me flash back to this time an IM popped up on my screen: "I saw you in the shower in gym. Guess what? I took your picture."

Immediately I deleted the three people on my buddy list. I'd only created that list because of a group project in history and someone suggested we talk on IM. So we wouldn't have to meet in person, of course. So they wouldn't be seen with me.

As soon as I got that message, my heart beat a hole in my chest. Oh my God, I thought. What if they put that picture on the Internet?

For weeks and weeks I searched. MySpace. Facebook. Twitter. I got so paranoid I couldn't go to school. I made myself sick with worry. I cried so much Mom called the doctor.

Like a doctor could fix me.

I hate IM. It takes all my willpower to add him to my buddy list. As I key "hervehotsu," my pulse races. "r u there?"

No response.

I let out a relieved breath. He's not online. Maybe the "O" is a zero. I try "herveh0tsu. u there?"

Nothing. Okay.

I stare at the blank screen.

For the hell of it, I key, "Can I borrow your laptop for a while? Not forever. This is . . ."

I key, "D."

I look at it. It reminds me how that girl changed my D to an A. It also reminds me of the last time someone called me D, and how I don't want to remember that—

I delete D and key "daelyn."

Before my nerves are shot, I hit ENTER.

- 12 DAYS, 11 DAYS -

Another reason I hate the weekends—it doesn't matter where I am or what I'm doing or how my parents attempt to distract me, I'm always alone with myself. The insults build in my brain until I'm ready to explode.

"Big fat farting pig."

"Fatso. Lardo. Chubette."

"Blimper. Heifer. Fudge pudge." I've heard them all. Some out loud. Some online.

The more I hurt, the more I ate. Yeah, I was a blimp. A doctor told me once I was twice as heavy at five feet tall as I should be. He said with a smile, "You know, there's a skinny person inside there trying to get out." He thought he was being helpful. He gave me the idea to kill two birds with one stone. Make that two people—one trapped inside the other.

The moving didn't help. Changing schools all the time. Kim and Chip rationalized it with Chip's job—new assignments, promotions. They were embarrassed by me, their sick, fat, psychotic creation. I should've figured out sooner how we moved every time I . . . what did Kim call it? Regressed? She got that one right out of the psychology text.

I call it wacked out. Exceeding my hypersensitivity limit. My limit is one nasty comment in the hall. "Double wide, step aside." While I slit my wrist, the voice plays over and

Over and

Over and

over and overand

overandoverand

overandoverandoverandoverandover and,

SHUT UP.

I didn't know what self-immolation was, at first.

Self-immolation

Effectiveness: 3–4.

Time: Seconds to days.

Availability: 2–3.

Pain: 5.

Notes: If you have access to gasoline and a match, you can easily set yourself on fire. This is, however, one of the most agonizing ways to die. If you survive, you will be disfigured for the rest of your life. It's recommended that you mix an explosive with the gasoline to make it burn much quicker. Make sure you're far away from medical help.

No way I'm getting into pyrotechnics. No flare for the dramatic, so to speak. The method I choose this time will have to leave no residue—no blood, no excrement, no ashes to ashes.

Drowning

Effectiveness: 3–4.

Time: 5 minutes to die of drowning; 20 minutes to die of hypothermia

Availability: 1.

Pain: 1.

Notes: Find deep (cold) water in a remote area. Weigh yourself down with rocks in your pockets. Tie your hands and legs together. You can be revived from cold water drowning after several hours, since the cold retards terminal brain damage. Warmer water does not have the advantage of hypothermia (loss of consciousness, thus pain), but is more effective in making sure you stay dead.

Very, very frightening.

Chip knocks and I jump. He pops his head in and says, "Were you on just now? I detected a user."

Casually, I darken the screen. As he's checking out my PC I reach for my paperback.

Chip goes, "Huh. It must be one of the neighbors. I thought the network was secure." He rubs the back of his neck as he leaves.

There's no lake or river nearby. But don't people die in bathtubs? Babies drown. Mothers drown their children. Didn't I read a person could drown in an inch of water?

It occupies my mind. Drowning, drowning, drowning. People drown in bathtubs. How scary could it be?

It doesn't have to be cold water. I hate the cold. Warm water would be soothing, relaxing. I could handle the panic. I would need to weigh myself down.

A plan crystallizes in my brain. It's like a vision.

Daelyn's Destiny.

About a week after we moved in, Chip said, "Why don't I build you a bookcase?"

He went to Lowe's and got planks and cinder blocks.

Kim said, "Why didn't you just buy a preassembled shelving unit?"

There was an awkward silence. Chip was forced to say it. "The metal strips are sharp."

Kim sucked in a breath.

The cinder blocks are perfect weights. I close my eyes and see it. Me, at the bottom of the bathtub with my hair flowing out in all directions. For once in my life, I'm beautiful.

- 10 DAYS -

He's not there after school. Good. Problem solved. I'll wear my brace to the end. I can read in bed by shifting from side to side for ten days. I can prop up on pillows. I can key in the Final Forum for short stretches of time. There's a lot to key still if I'm going to tell everything, but ten days is an eternity.

Out of nowhere he appears, lugging a stack of laptops. The sight of him makes my breathing speed up. He plops down beside me. "I have three for you to choose from"—Hervé is draped around his neck—"depending on what you want to do. If you're a gamer, this Dell has a two-gig Core Duo, another gig of RAM, and a screaming video card." He sets it on my lap.

Why? Why would he . . . ?

"This LG has a blinding screen, but the snakeskin is cool. It comes with a wad of junkware you'll never use." He slides it on top of the first computer. My thighs feel the weight.

He can't be serious.

"This Samsung, which I call the Mini Me, has touch screen and a fingerprint scanner, if you're security minded.

Plus, at two pounds it's ultralight. I just got it."

He balances the computer on top. It's the one he was fooling with the other day. Hervé scrabbles around so he's facing me, his beady eyes boring into my nostrils.

I want to ask him a vital question. Not the rat.

"I got the first two on Craigslist."

That's not it.

"The Mini Me was an early birthday present. Ask me why."

I don't care. But why would you give me . . . ?

"They're Wi-Fi, of course."

That's it. As long as I have Internet access, I can get to Through-the-Light.

He waits a minute, looking smug. Just for that I decide to take his new one.

"Phenomenal choice. Enjoy the tunes I've downloaded. You can borrow my periphs too, if you want. Or anything else."

He's not supposed to be happy about it.

He won't get anything from me. I should tell him the truth, that I don't put out, that I never will no matter how nice he seems or how generous or desperate.

But damn. I want this laptop.

I slide it into my book bag at my feet, retrieve *Desire on the Moor* and a pen. I write in the margin, I ONLY NEED IT FOR 10 DAYS. I'LL PAY YOU 5 DOLLARS A DAY.

He reads the note and goes, "Make it ten dollars."

A hundred dollars? Forget it. I reach down to grab the laptop, and his hand spreads over mine. Reflexively, I snatch my hand away.

"I'm kidding," he says. "I don't want your money."

Which means I'm right about what he does want.

He adds, "Just IM me. Okay?"

I really want the laptop. OK I lie.

He sets the rejected computers on the bench beside him—the other side of him—pulls a paperback from his pocket and scoots closer. DON'T. I stick him in the arm with my pen.

"Ouch," he goes, but scoots away. "Stab me, why don't you?"

My pleasure.

He rubs his arm. "I didn't know if you had the next book in the series, so I got it. Thought I'd start at the end and work backward." He opens the back cover of his book.

I recognize it. *Desire in the Mine.*

He settles in to read.

Now I can't read. He's . . . unnerving.

I sit there faking it, with a rat snarling at me.

"Amazing," he says. "Compelling. Intriguing. What I don't understand is what Charles is getting out of this relationship. Maggie Louise is a slut."

No, she's not! I shoot him a fiery glare, which he deflects with the book in front of his face.

Okay, she is. But she gets what she wants in the end.

"Do you know the girl in your school with the long black hair and bangs?" he asks.

Does he mean JenniferJessica?

"She has a blue streak down one side."

JenniferJessica.

He goes, "She reminds me of Maggie Louise."

What? I shift to look at him, but he's reading intently, smiling.

She's nothing like Maggie Louise. How well does he know JenniferJessica? I want to tell him, She's not your type. How do I know what type he is? What boy wouldn't desire someone like JenniferJessica?

He's yanking my chain. I hate him.

Kim arrives. I pack my gear and head for the car. This time he doesn't follow. Good.

"What's in your bag?" Kim asks as I meld with the bucket seat and latch my seat belt. "Can I see?" She extends her hand.

I must clutch my bag tighter because Kim retracts her arm. "That's okay. I trust you."

She'll check it later.

As we're driving away, I watch Santana loping up the steps to the house next door. The computers are slung under his arm and Hervé is riding his shoulder.

"Is that where he lives?" Kim asks.

He turns and waves.

I want to wave back, but . . . I catch myself.

We slow for a yellow light and I don't know why, but I turn my torso and look back to see if he's still there.

Kim says, "You like him. I can tell."

I shut down. You can't tell anything.

The little laptop, the Mini Me, is great. My fingers adjust to the stiff keyboard right away.

The Internet connection is automatic. I wonder if Chip can detect a new user or an added piece of hardware. At this point, I don't really care. He can't get into Through-the-Light.

I lie in bed and log on.

Three J_Doe's have replied to my last Final Forum entry. People have been verbally and physically abused. Fag is a standard. Dyke, slut, homo, whore, Arab. That's a new one. One girl was called . . . I don't even want to say it. By her mother, no less.

Purge, I think. Get rid of it. I switch over to *Sexual Assault*. The last entry is by J_Doe022292: *They got me. The boys who were after me. They got me after school and beat and raped me.*

I key, "He waited for me, to walk me to my locker. Every day for a week. He even said, 'Hey, D. I've been waiting for you.'"

My breath comes in deep, rasping gulps. It all comes rushing back. "His friends called him Toomey. He was popular. He always had crowds of people around him, girls especially."

So why would he choose a girl like me? If I could've seen through my delusional state at the time, I'd have known. We didn't talk. He just took my backpack, slung it over his shoulder, and walked with me.

So cool.

"I couldn't believe he was walking with me. When people passed us, he'd wave. I'd hear them snicker behind our backs, but he didn't seem to care. He liked me for who I was."

How stupid. He didn't know who I was. How could he?

"He'd leave me at my locker and lean in like he was going to kiss me. He'd say in this sexy voice, 'Thank you for our special time, D.'"

I'd wish and pray, Kiss me. Go ahead. You can if you want.

I'd never been kissed by a boy. Ever since elementary, girls were always bragging about how boys kissed them and gave them rings. It seemed every girl in the world had had a boyfriend by then except me.

The memory of Toomey jolts me back to reality and I double over, holding my stomach. But it hurts my neck and I feel like throwing up. I hunch over the computer and key rapid fire, "The day it happened I was in the lunch line and people were butting in front of me. I let them. I always let them. I had to go back to my locker because I forgot my lunch money, and he was there. Toomey. With his friends. They were older boys, eighth graders. They started elbowing each other when they saw me coming, and Toomey called, 'Yo, D. Whassup?' My heart fluttered. I spoke the first words I'd ever spoken to him: 'I forgot my lunch money.'"

"'Oh, yeah?'

"He came up behind me and spun me around. He took the five dollar bill I'd gotten from my purse and held it over my head. When I reached for it, he yanked it away. He was grinning. I started giggling and going, 'Give it to me,' and he said, 'Come and get it, D.' He backed up and up and I followed him all the way to the door of the boys' restroom. He went in and I stopped.

"Suddenly I was surrounded by Toomey's gang. They pushed me in through the door. I was squealing, but more like girls do when boys are teasing them, because I thought it was just a game."

It was supposed to be a game!

"Inside the bathroom, one guy blocked the door and another shoved me forward. 'Go on, Toomey,' one of them said. 'Kiss her. You said she wants it.' He held my arms in back. Toomey smiled—make that leered—then leaned in so close I could smell his sour breath. The other guys chanted, 'Do it, do it. . . .' I looked at Toomey and his eyes changed to black."

He scared me. It was like he changed into a different person. A monster.

"He leaned in to kiss me, but I turned away. He grabbed my chin and smashed his lips on mine so hard it bent my head and I hit the wall. The guys all had me pinned against the wall while Toomey swiped off his lips, like the taste of me was disgusting. He spit into the sink, and went, 'Who's next?'"

I broke away and ran for the door, but they got me.

"I tried to scream, but a hand clamped over my mouth. Someone felt my boob and said, 'Hey, there's a lot under there.' He squeezed so hard it hurt. 'Toomey, you said you wondered what a fatty paddy looks like naked.' At the sink, Toomey eyed me up and down."

I struggled with all my might to twist free, but the guys were strong and determined.

"One guy lifted up my blouse, and they all went, 'Whoa.' My bra strap had broken in the struggle. For a second their grips loosened, and I made a run for the door, but someone caught my skirt, so I swung around and dodged into a toilet stall. A hand grabbed my leg and I slipped on the wet floor and fell and they tried to drag me out, but I held on to the toilet and they couldn't. I felt my skirt being lifted up and I flattened myself on the floor and squeezed my legs together. One of them said, 'Let's go, dude. Leave her be.' Toomey snapped, 'I say when we go.' He tried to pull down my underwear, but he couldn't get it very far."

Please go, I prayed. I smashed my face to the toilet basin and shut my eyes, praying to God.

"Toomey put his foot on my rear and said, 'Blubber butt.' I felt pressure, like he was going to crush me. 'Rat us out and we'll kill you, pig.' The stall door slammed shut."

As my hands lift off the keyboard, they're shaking.

The guys laughed. Each one smacked the stall door before they left. Then I was alone, trembling and wheezing and pulling up my pants.

That goes beyond bullying. It's always what you're scared of—what they might do to you physically.

What they *will* do if you ever trust anyone.

I look up at the monitor, where J_Doe030393 has written: *I got raped by my stepdad and his friend.*

What they did wasn't rape, but I felt violated.

I'm still back there. Sticky pee on the floor and I'm stuck to it.

I smell the pee on my hands sometimes. My fingers stick together. Sometimes I have to wash my hands until they're scraped clean and raw.

J_Doe030393 goes on: *He'd lock the door after everyone went to bed. I couldn't tell on him. He said he'd take me out in a field and kill me. I wish he had.*

If you're here, he did kill you.

I'm caught between then and now. I can't leave and I can't move forward. They jammed the stall so hard it wouldn't open. I have to crawl underneath to get out, and I'm stuck, I'm so fat. At last I writhe and wiggle myself free. I find my class in the lunch line and Toomey is there, talking to my teacher. "Her." He points. "She was in the boys' bathroom. I've seen her in there before hiding in the stall to watch us guys take a piss. She's a perv."

My teacher starts yelling. What I see in my nightmares are all the eyes on me. White eyes in black space.

Lines scroll across the monitor. J_Doe021594 has written: *My father used to lock me in the cellar on Sundays. He'd get drunk and come at me with a belt. He'd strap my back until I was bloody, then tie me up and rape me.*

Terror.

I was terrorized too.

One girl from my class said, "Ew, you stink" and they all backed away from me. I was holding my hands out in front and they were filthy and reeked of urine. The next thing I know I'm in the principal's office and she's demanding to know why I was in the boys' restroom. I can't tell her because . . . I can't. She calls my mom. *Perv perv perv perv perv perv*, all the voices jam together.

STOP.

J_Doe022786 writes: *In my middle school there's this initiation or hazing ritual I guess you call it where the 7th graders, the sevies, get their heads dunked in dirty toilet bowls for swirlies. While someone held down my head, though, someone else yanked down my pants. He shoved a pencil up my ass. That wasn't part of the initia-*

tion. I was a chosen sevie.

We're all chosen here.

On that day, like all the others, Mom came to pick me up. I know she wasn't happy about being called away from work again. I hear her exhale the exasperation.

She asks, "What happened this time, Daelyn?"

I start to cry.

The principal says, "Apparently she sneaks into the boys' restroom."

"No, I don't!"

Mom looks down on me.

I sniffle and try to calm myself. "They pushed me in. They locked me in a stall." I can't describe the rest. *Please, Mom, don't make me.*

Mom says to the principal, "Why would she sneak into the boys' restroom?"

The principal doesn't reply, like the answer is obvious.

Mom hesitates for a long minute. Then she says, "I believe Daelyn. She's never lied to me."

I hadn't, up to then. I'd just never told her the whole truth.

The principal asks me, "Do you know who did it? Can you identify the boys?"

That's when the roaring starts in my ears.

"Tell me!" the principal demands. "Tell me who did it." She's screaming at me, like the whole thing is my fault. I have to cover my ears.

Mom squats down to be eye level with me and takes my hands away from my ears. "We can't help you, honey, unless you tell us who it was."

I swallow hard. In a tiny voice, I say, "I don't remember."

"I think you do," the principal says accusingly.

Mom's squeezing my shoulders, clenching my arms so tight she's squeezing the life out of me. "Tell us, Daelyn. Tell me."

The consequence of ratting them out . . . Not only that, but the humiliation. It was a game. Play the fat girl.

The principal says, "You've never reported any of this to the mediators. I don't have one report." She tells Mom, "We have a student mediator program to handle bullying."

How ridiculous. You expect people to police themselves?

The principal adds, "We have a zero tolerance policy."

Zero tolerance for the truth.

In the car on the way home, I broke down completely. Mom said, "Daelyn, for heaven's sake. Will you stop crying? It was a silly prank. Maybe those boys tease you because secretly they like you." She smiled at me.

I almost threw up.

Mom said, "Just forget it. It's all over now."

It'll never be over.

She added, "Let's not tell your father, okay? You know how he gets."

I didn't tell him. And I never told her the whole truth. What would it matter? There was nothing she could do; nothing anyone can do or will do.

An IM pops up on the screen.

hervehOtsu: Yo D. Whassup?

I power down.

- 9 DAYS -

He's waiting for me at the gate, which he's never done. His arms are crossed and he looks pissed.

What?

I stand behind the gate and wait. He doesn't move or speak. Fine.

I open the gate and he has to step out of my way as I come through. He says, "If you're not going to communicate with me, I want my laptop back."

I don't respond.

"Come on," he says, steepling his hands in a plea. "Please?"

His eyes are deep, dark blue, and it startles me to a stop. I can't notice the color of his eyes. Ducking my head, I scuttle to the bench.

He says, "My last friend from around here moved to Germany, and everyone else in my long distance learning school lives out of state. I don't know them anyway. I'm lonely." He's wearing flip-flops and his toenails are painted purple. I didn't know boys painted their nails. I didn't know they got lonely. But it explains why he's talking to me, at least partly.

He stands there and I take the laptop out of my bag.

"Does it work okay?" he asks. "Do you need me to come over and install anything?"

I hand it to him, but he won't take it.

"You said you need it for ten days, so I'm keeping track. Why ten days?"

When I sigh wearily, he collapses on the ground at my feet, bending one knee to his chest and looping an arm around it.

He has facial fuzz, kind of sketchy looking. He's cute—for a dork. Too cute for me. I clench the laptop to my chest and close up inside, like the clam I am.

"Did you get my IM?"

I don't know why I'm trembling and my breathing is uneven. With shaky hands, I exchange the laptop for my book. I open to chapter thirteen. *Maggie Louise tapped lightly on Jean-Jacques's door. At this hour, midnight, the manor was alive with noises of the night. The grandfather clock ticking in the parlor; a breeze off the moor clattering a loose shutter; ghosts of roomers swirling up the staircase and clashing in the hall. Maggie Louise's senses were heightened, and when Jean-Jacques opened the door, all her desires awakened.*

Maggie Louise would never allow herself to be violated.

He lets go of his leg and peers off to the side.

Look, I think. I didn't ask you to come here. I don't care if your feelings are hurt or you're disappointed, or you think you can't even attract a fat, ugly, mute girl.

I don't care. I don't care.

"I have Hodgkin's lymphoma," he says.

104

My breath catches. Isn't that cancer?

"I was in remission and thought I had it beat, then right before my last follow-up, I found a lump."

He's making this up.

"Relapses almost always occur within the first two years. Almost. Always . . ." His voice trails away.

I'm not looking at him, even though the sun is shining on his face and glistening in his hair. His head falls back and his toes stretch up. "I'm not telling you this so you'll feel sorry for me."

He snags my eye and arches his eyebrows. "Unless that works."

Everyone's a liar. Everyone I've ever known. He's lying about the cancer.

Twenty-three J_Doe's on the DOD today. Twenty-three completers. Kim pokes her head in. "Your father's working late, so it'll just be us for dinner. Where'd you get that?"

I shut the lid and set the laptop aside on my bed. "Did Santana give it to you?" Yes, Kim. Because he's in love with me. He finds me beautiful and desirable.

I'm the biggest liar of all.

I scoot off the edge of the mattress and Kim says, "You're not wearing your brace."

I walk to my desk and open a drawer. It's empty. My book bag is slung over the back of the rocking chair, and I go over to it, dig around for what I need. A pen. The back of a math problem sheet I never bothered to start. I write: "Can I take a walk?" I hand it to Kim.

She reads the note. "Where?"

I set the pen on the desk and gaze into my blank monitor.

Kim looks at me, down at the note, up at me. She lowers the note to her side and goes, "I don't suppose you want me to walk with you."

I feel her eyes, her overarching need to reach me. I'm too far gone.

"Okay," she says. "But I'm going to follow you."

I check the clock on the mantel before leaving the house. Timing is everything. When and how. The route to school is mapped in my head. Right on 26th Avenue. Left on Wadsworth Boulevard. Three miles, approximately, to Alameda and the Belmar Shopping Center, then two blocks east to St. Mary's.

It's twenty minutes by car. What I need to know is how long it will take me on foot to get home from school.

I didn't realize Kim meant she was going to follow me in the car.

She putters along behind, pulling into driveways or side streets every few minutes to let traffic pass. One guy honks and flips her the bird.

Flip him back, Kim.

She just takes it.

A new Walgreens is going up at the halfway point. My feet hurt. I should've changed out of my school loafers. Except they're the only shoes I have now.

Kim draws up alongside me and rolls down the passenger window, "Where are you going, Daelyn?"

She doesn't know the route by now?

106

"What are you doing?"

Clocking time, Kim.

You won't know until it's over. You won't find me in time.

I suppose I could do it at night, drug them before they go to bed, but like I said, I don't have access to drugs. Anyway, drugs are unpredictable. I might kill them, and that is not my intent.

No, this time they won't even think to check on me. They'll both be at work.

The Comfort Dental sign rises in the distance. My throat is dry and my legs ache. This is more physical exertion than my body is used to. Worthless shell of a body. I hope they cremate it.

Don't keep the urn.

Finally I see the school. The fence around St. Mary's Academy. A raw cough rips my vocal cords—what's left of them.

"Hey." His voice carries across the street. "Daelyn." In my peripheral vision, I see him launch off a hammock on his porch and lope toward me. He seems perfectly fine. He isn't sick. He has that stupid rat in his hand.

"Whassup?" He falls into step beside me. I'm moving again. I'm half a block from the gate.

I panic. There's a flaw in my plan. I don't have a watch. Time means nothing, except for now.

I whirl and frantically jab at my wrist. Santana frowns. Then he gets it, because he says, "I don't know. I don't wear a watch."

Damn. DAMN.

Kim's CR-V chugs to the curb. I rush over and lean my head in the window. Five forty-eight on the car clock. My breathing slows. I calculate: An hour and thirteen minutes. Add three minutes from the girls' restroom by the office where I'll wait for the all clear to leave.

I'll have to go to first period, to make sure my attendance is recorded. Then I'll write a note to my teacher that my throat feels swollen and I have to go to the office to call my mom.

"You don't look so hot," he says. "I mean, you always look hot. But you look all red and puffy."

I hack a dry cough.

"Are you all right?"

I bend over to wheeze in a lung-filling breath.

He touches my back.

Don't touch me!

"Daelyn?" Kim calls out the window. A door slams.

My arm is yanked backward, pulling me, my body across the street and onto the bench. He hovers over me.

I can't catch my breath.

"You need water?" he asks.

I'm gasping.

"Here, hold Hervé." The rat drops in my lap.

"I'll run in and get her some water," I hear him say. "Does she have asthma or something? Do you have an inhaler?"

Kim says, "Water. Yes. Thank you."

There's a rat in my lap. A silent scream claws up my chest and constricts my breathing even more. The rat leaps onto my shoulder and a *scree* sounds in my ears. Is that me? The scaly tail tickles my arm.

Kim stands there.

Take it! I want to scream. Get it off me.

"Does it bite?" she asks.

How do I know? The whiskers tickle my neck.

Kim lowers herself to the bench, keeping her distance. "Why didn't you ask me to drive you here if you needed to come back to school?" She sounds mad.

"Did you forget some homework?" She lets out a little shriek as the rat leaps into her lap.

I'm wheezing and shaking all over. I might be dying.

"Here we go." He gallops up with a plastic cup, which he thrusts in my face. He lifts my spazzing arm to take it. The cup is slimy, like water sloshed out and mixed with his sweaty hand.

Holding my hand, he raises the cup to my lips.

Stop touching me.

Oh, God. Liquid.

I swig the whole cup of cold water.

"Better?"

He takes his hand away and I blink yes.

"You can pet him," he says to Kim. "In fact, here. He loves to have his belly rubbed." Santana plucks the rat off Kim's lap and upends him; stretches him out lengthwise in front of Kim.

I can breathe again.

"That's okay," Kim goes. "I don't care to touch him."

I smile inwardly as she flattens herself against the back of the bench.

"Awww." Santana lifts the rat to his face and nuzzles his stomach. "The ladies are not appreciating your rockin' rat dudeness, my man." He loops Hervé over his head and onto his shoulders.

I'm not watching, really. I'm still feeling the soothing liquid sliding down my throat as I press the cool cup to my forehead.

Kim scoots closer and loops an arm across my shoulder. I feel the heaviness. Don't feel. I can't look at her because I know what I'll see.

Helplessness, weakness, a reflection of me.

"Oh. Here." Santana digs something out of his pocket and drops it in my lap. An energy bar. "Ariel buys these by the case."

Kim twists her head up to Santana. "Thank you." She stands. She appears to compose herself. "We were on our way to Dairy Queen."

No. I know what she's going to do.

"Would you like to join us?"

I spring to my feet and the energy bar flies. I shove the cup at Santana and head for the car.

He says, loud enough for me to hear, "Thanks, but I promised Ariel I'd wait for her. It's my night to cook."

Kim's footsteps behind me. Santana's too. "Hey, you should go to On the Border in Belmar. Ask to sit in Ariel's section. Order the guac. While she's making it at the table, tell her Santana says a little heavy on the cilantro, hon." I turn and see him grin.

I don't care who Ariel is. Ariel who?

"Rain check?" Santana says to Kim.

"Definitely." She smiles.

I get in the car.

He licks his index finger and sticks it in the air. "Low pressure trough dropping down from the north. Cold wave expected to move in by midnight. Bundle up, ladies."

Through the window, he hands me the energy bar. His eyes, his slight smile. I take it. Santana goes softly, "Hervé says eat more, skinnybones."

I'm not that skinny. I'm not fat anymore, but I'm not skinny. I'll never be skinny. I went to fat camp. We're not going to talk about what happened there. I was *forced* to go. I still feel fat. I'll always be fat and ugly.

I navigate to the Final Forum, to *Bullied*. I need to open the closet now and release that fear.

"My mom thought moving would help," I key. "Moving only made it worse because I was the new FAT girl. Boys jostle me in the hall. They come up behind me and go *quack quack, waddle waddle*. One calls me Krispy Kreme."

They make me sick.

"One morning, this was at the beginning of 5th grade, they said, 'Come over here. We want to show you something.' I didn't trust them, but then they said, 'It's a secret. You can't tell anyone.' Like they wanted me to be one of them, or something. How naïve am I? The janitor's door was open and when I peeked in they shoved me inside and the steel door clanged shut. It locked automatically. I couldn't turn the knob. I pounded on the door and yelled, 'This isn't funny. Let me out.'

"Time passed, like ten or twenty minutes. 'Help!' I yelled. 'I'm in here. Someone is locked in here. Get me out.'"

111

The odor in that closet pinches my nose. I can't get rid of it—still.

J_Doe061171 writes: *My friend—exfriend—started a rumor that I was a lesbian and someone spray painted the side of my car with DYKE.*

I key, "The closet reeked of ammonia and vomit. I screamed, 'HELP! HELP ME!'"

I close my eyes and I'm there, panicking. There's no light. All I can see are shadows moving, like spiders and rats and more rats.

I was in there for hours. Pounding on the door. I had to pee so bad. I couldn't hold it.

J_Doe090192 writes: *I'm scard to leave my hous. Everone is after me. I've been dignosed parinoid schizofrenac, but I'm not. I kno there after me.*

"Finally," I key, "like eight hours later, the janitor opened the door. He had a cop and the principal with him. And my mom and dad."

I stood on wobbly legs. "Oh, Daelyn." I can still hear the pity in Mom's voice. "What happened this time?"

She blames me. I'm delirious from the ammonia fumes and the pounding and my hands are all bloody and she blames me. Daddy picks me up, bodily, and grunts with the weight.

I was still fat back then. I felt cold and wet on my legs.

I key, "I feel the chill on my legs. My dad says, 'You're wet. She's all wet,' he announces to the world. I about die of embarrassment. Yes, I peed my pants."

J_Doe090878 writes: *Bad stuff happens in the dark. Evil lurks behind closed doors.*

Oh, that's deep. You're a real philosopher.

Is anyone here listening?

I pound the keyboard, taking my anger and frustration out on it. "My mom says, 'Have you been in here all day?' 'Yes,' I tell her. She screams at the janitor, 'Didn't anyone even notice she was missing?'"

That same piercing screech in her voice every time at the hospital. "Do something!" When I slit my wrists. "Help her!" The last time too. "Somebody help her. *Help us!*"

You're helpless, both of you. All of us.

J_Doe040595 writes: *My father molested me when I was six.*

Put that in *Sexual Assault*! Can't these people read?

I start to key the rest, then give up. Who cares anyway? We had a sub that day and no one told her I was missing. Krispy Kreme. I take a deep breath and lie back on my pillow. Being locked in a closet is nothing. Pissing yourself is nothing. Sitting in your own pee and ammonia and vomit, your fingers caked with blood, inconsequential.

I shouldn't have been there. I should never have been born.

By the time I was ten I already knew my destiny. By middle school I had a plan for escape, for control. There's always a way out. All you have to do is take it.

- 8 DAYS -

A question appears on my monitor:

How will you get to the light?

What does that mean? What's my mode of transportation? Spirit Express.

I assume you just go. You float or fly or evaporate. You get sucked into a vortex. You shoot out of your body. You spiral or propel. The angels sing you up.

I don't believe in angels. There was a time I did. I even talked to God. While I was slitting my wrists, I said to God, "Take me. Please. Deliver me from evil."

When God didn't, it made me question my faith. What little I had.

The second time, I made it clear. I threatened God. "Okay, listen. If you save me again, I'll hate you. I'll never forgive you and I'll stop believing."

God doesn't listen.

I keep my promises.

How will you get to the light? Maybe I'm overthinking it. They want to know my method. Way to Go.

I key in, "Drowning."

* * *

At breakfast Chip says, "That new laptop is password-protected. Will you give me your password?"

I guess Kim told him about it. I should've told Kim, "Let's not let Chip in on our dirty little secret."

Chip adds, "I won't read your story."

"What story?" Kim asks.

"She's working on a story. For English, is it?"

I suck in a spoonful of oatmeal.

Kim swigs her coffee. "If she's talking to Santana, that's okay. They're friends." She smiles at me.

I stir my slime.

A long minute passes.

"So, write down your password before you leave." Chip gets up to load his dishes into the dishwasher.

I almost salute. I'll give him my password, but he won't get in. I'm fingerprint protected.

He's lying on the bench, his hands under his head. He's barefoot. His flip-flops are on the grass and he's wearing those camo shorts that hang on him. He shaved today. He even doused with aftershave that smells like lime.

A person with cancer doesn't care about aftershave.

"Did you see the fogbow this morning?" he asks. "I bet you know about fogbows. It's uncommon knowledge, but you're an uncommon person."

What a line. He doesn't look at me not looking or listening to him.

"I have a sixth sense about people," he says. "Or it might

be a seventh sense. I knew it from the first time I saw you, here on my bench, under this magnolia tree."

There's no such thing as a seventh sense. It's *my* bench.

"Fogbows are rainbows in the fog. But you knew that. You have to look hard to see one. You have to know what you're looking for."

He's so full of shit.

It rained all night. He was right about the rain. Thick fog this morning.

I stand at the end of the bench, tapping my foot. Finally he swings his legs down and sits upright. He teeters and clenches the front of the bench. "Whoa," he goes.

I sit. I take out my book and open to my bookmark.

Maggie Louise zipped up her jodhpurs and said to Charles, "I'm off for my riding lesson."

Charles peered over his book. "Do you think you should ride in this fog?"

"Ariel's my mom, as you no doubt figured out if you went to On the Border. I don't want you consumed with jealous rage, thinking I have women all over town."

I raise the book to my face to hide any trace of a smile. He's so *not* the stud he thinks he is.

"There's only one girl in my life." He pushes to his feet.

He's leaving?

"Maggie Louise."

Who will see you through the darkness?

He's funny. Dorky, but funny. If he really had cancer, wouldn't it show? Wouldn't he be bald or stuck in bed? My

116

sickness is invisible, except when I fail and have to wear a neck brace.

I press ENTER, but it won't let me bypass the question.

Who will see you through the darkness?

It won't be God. These questions are annoying. What do they mean? Who's asking?

Kim won't see me through, I hope, if I'm looking back through the darkness. Although she'll be the one to find me. She'll drive up to St. Mary's after school and see I'm not where I'm supposed to be. Maybe he'll be there. With Hervé, of course.

Hervé Villechaize Junior. In another life I might find that amusing. He watches reruns of *Fantasy Island*, like I used to. In another life I might not be terrified of rats.

He'll say, "I haven't seen her, Mrs. R. I thought she might be sick today."

She only lets me stay home sick when I really am physically ill. I always go. I take it and take it and take it.

Kim will say, "I dropped her off at school." Checkpoint A. "I saw her go into the building." Each day I'm her burden, she waits until I'm inside. She watches me open the gate, close it, walk up the wide path, climb the four marble steps, grab the iron handle, pull open the door, step inside. She waves. The last day, I think, I should wave back.

No. That'd stick in her memory.

If I'm Chip's duty that day, my DOD, he'll probably drive off before I enter the building. He usually trusts that I'll make it inside once I'm through the gate.

There's a teacher at the door to check IDs and book bags.

We must carry the official St. Mary's book bag. It's dark blue with the gold seal. You can convert it to a backpack or carry it like a tote.

I never got a choice because my neck brace dictated tote.

The first thing I always do every morning is go to the chapel. I get dropped off in plenty of time to make it to class, and I'm not about to hang out in the courtyard with the other girls. All the JenniferJessicas.

Girls scare me more than boys. Boys are cruel. Girls are mean.

One time in art we had to pair up to draw portraits. When was this, seventh grade? This girl, whose name I don't remember and don't care to, got stuck with me. She was pretty, or would've been if she didn't scowl the whole time. My portrait of her was good. I took care with it. When she showed me mine, my face flushed. The roaring of people's laughter swelled in my ears.

She'd drawn this hideous blob with bandages on both wrists.

It was her way of saying, "You should kill yourself."

In the chapel, I sit in a pew and look out the stained-glass window. Last week the window was cranked wide open. Why, I don't know. To air out the evil?

Suddenly he's there. Santana. Across the yard, standing at the wrought-iron fence. A bunch of girls are milling around in the courtyard and he calls to them. They turn.

One breaks away from the pack. JenniferJessica.

Why is he talking to her? Why is she smiling and

flipping her hair over her shoulder? She's not your type! I want to scream.

Like I care. What do I care?

Who will see you through the darkness? Not Santana, unless he has X-ray vision. Which he obviously doesn't.

I'll have to go to econ first period. Suffer through roll call.

I've scoped out the school. A person can easily slip out through Gregory Hall and skim the hedges between buildings. Around the chapel, the cafeteria, make a run for the gate.

Now JenniferJessica is walking away. She rejoins her crew and they put their heads together. I can guess what they're saying, how they think his ears are big, how he babbles about the weather. So what? They don't know him. They wouldn't take the time.

The gate is never locked. That's symbolic, I suppose. Like the gates of heaven are always open to us.

By 9:12 a.m., I'll be on my way.

My mind drifts and I'm gone for a while. When I wake up, the story fast-forwards.

Santana's gone.

Kim will be concerned that I'm late. After school. She'll check the clock in the car. She'll debate with herself: Get out and go inside? Wait a few more minutes? Call Chip and ask him what to do?

Santana might say, "I didn't see her all day, Mrs. R." If he's still there, if he's on my bench. If he's been standing at the fence, flirting with JenniferJessica.

She could give him what he wants. She won't, but

she could. He'd believe every word that came out of a JenniferJessica's mouth. Because he's desperate. Naïve. Then she'd drop him like a stink bomb.

This isn't about him, because he's not dying and I don't care.

Thinking I walked, Kim might drive slowly. Chip might beat her home. Doubtful, since his office is clear across town. No, it'll be Kim. She'll call Chip to let him know what she's doing. She might tell Santana, "Call me if she shows up, okay?" She'll give him her cell number.

She'll park in the carport, Slot A, 3996 Indiana Street. She'll grab her briefcase and lunch bag, or maybe she'll leave them behind in her rush. Her shoes will crunch the gravel in the patio. She'll find the back door locked.

If Chip beats her there—say he left immediately and tore home, it's possible he would find me first—he'll call, "Daelyn, are you here?"

My stomach twists a little. I won't be alive so I won't care who finds me. In the bathtub all gray and bloated, a cinder block on my face.

It disturbs me a little that Chip might think he had something to do with it. I'm sorry, Dad. If it hadn't been cinder blocks I would've found other weights.

I squelch the guilt.

Who will see you through the darkness?

"Me," I key in the answer. "I'll find my own way."

It's hell dredging up these memories, but I need to purge. Remembering is costing me, though, by bringing back feelings. There's only a week to cleanse, so I take a deep breath and key, "The summer between 7th and 8th grades, I lost 22 pounds at fat camp." Just typing "fat camp" makes me sick. Maybe I should call it fitness camp.

But I didn't come back fit to live.

A message appears on my screen: *That password didn't work. Are you sure it's 123XYZ?*

Chip figured out my new IM name. I stare at his message for a minute, then IM him back, "I saved to autofill and can't remember now."

He'll keep trying, over and over.

I message him, "I'm just working on my story. OK?"

He writes back, "I can't wait to read it."

I hope he never finds this forum after I'm gone.

"After camp I grew a couple of inches. I went from 5′ 0″ to 5′ 2″. And I lost 50 more pounds. My mom was like, 'You look lovely. The boys will be lining up now,' and Dad was like, 'You're growing up too fast. What happened to my little girl?'"

She died, Chip.

If a final ray of hope had been flickering inside me, it was snuffed out at fat camp. There's no reason to remember. No purpose served by reliving that horror.

So many bullying incidents to record. Like, the first day of eighth grade, these three girls walk by me at my locker and they all turn their heads. They're clones. One of them curls a lip. She says something to her look-alikes and they all cackle. In unison, they form L's on their foreheads with their fingers.

J_Doe111191 writes: *Where is fat camp?*

In hell, I almost reply.

121

Someone is listening; someone actually read and absorbed what I wrote. I key, "In Arizona."

J_Doe090384 writes: *My parents sent me away to boarding school when I was eleven. They never came to visit not even on parents' weekend. They didn't care if I ever came home again.*

I sigh and resume my story. "I knew right then and there nothing was ever going to change. It wouldn't matter if I was tall or short or fat or thin or absent every day. I was a loser from birth."

I stop keying. Only one other person is logged on.

I'm about to log off when J_Doe111191 writes: *me 2.*

I've kept the empty book covers to populate my bookshelf and divert suspicion. When I disassemble the bookcase to carry the cinder blocks to the bathroom, I'll toss the last of the trash into a Glad bag with the final remnants of my room. No muss. No fuss.

I decide to leave the bathroom door wide open when I do it. So I can breathe. Which makes no sense at all. I guess I have a phobia about being closed in.

I can't sleep. In the dark, I open the laptop and it flashes awake. Black and white. I fingerprint access.

There's a pop-up message: *I wish you'd IM me. I need your advice. Santana.*

About what?

How'd he pop up like that? I wasn't even on IM. I stare at the screen for a while, baffled. He must be an evil genius or something. It is his machine, so maybe he can link to it anytime.

If I IM him back, he'll know I'm using his machine. He'll think I'm open to communicating. I don't want to lead him on.

I log on to Through-the-Light. There's a message with a red flag: *Updates have been made to WTG.*

So? I've already chosen drowning. Maybe it knows I haven't considered every option. How could it know?

There's another question too.

What awaits you?

Meaning?

I try to skip it, but the question keeps repeating.

What awaits you?

What awaits you?

Okay. Here's what I picture: This plume of warm air sweeps me up and drops me at the gate. Not a pearly gate, or an ornamental gate. A metaphoric gate. My spirit, or soul, or consciousness enters a spectral arena and I see the light. It's an orb in the distance, like a shiny dime.

I walk along a cobbled path. There are others, but we don't speak. They have their own paths to take. Everyone is silent, respectful. Which is nice. For once. At last, up here, I can close my eyes and not see all the scenes playing out, not feel the crushing weight of life. No one has eyes. There's sight within me. I have, like, insight or farsight.

That's too much to key in. I type, "Eternal peace. Serenity."

The answer is acceptable.

Two J_Doe's are on the DOD list. A light travel day, I guess. I link to WTG.

Starvation/Dehydration

Effectiveness: 5, if not force-fed.

Time: Approximately 40 days.

Availability: 1.

Pain: 3–5.

Notes: Theoretically easier after the first two days. A living will or durable power of attorney may prevent relatives from intervening once you're unconscious. An appetite suppressant such as amphetamines or ecstasy is recommended. Fatal dehydration can be extremely painful.

I don't have forty days. Anyway, the irony of me starving to death . . .

Freezing to Death

Time: 15 minutes in very cold water to several hours in a freezer.

I hate being cold.

I scroll to the newest entries at the bottom.

Jumping in Front of a Train

Note: Terrifying. Best to lay your neck on the track, since a break in your spine may only cripple you for life.

Not an option.

Getting Someone to Murder You

I don't know anyone who'd do that for me.

Getting Eaten Alive

By what? I skip to the notes: *Ants or carnivores such as large cats . . .*

I shudder. You'd have to live in a jungle.

Kim sticks her head in the door. "You already up?"

I power down. It's morning.

She comes in and sits on my mattress. "Your throat must

be feeling better. You're not wearing your brace."

The brace is to support my throat until it heals. But there is no healing me.

I close the lid of the laptop.

"So, did Santana give you that laptop?"

I could nod, but I choose not to engage.

"I'm glad you have a friend." Kim touches my hand, then actually takes it in hers. "Do we need to have *the talk?*" Her eyebrows arch.

All my muscles contract.

Kim laughs at the expression on my face, I guess. She goes, "I don't even want to know what you're looking up on the Internet." There's a long pause, and I think my mother is the most clueless person in the world. "But if you have questions about intercourse, or birth control, you know you can ask me, right?"

Oh, sure. Because we always talk about deep down stuff.

I'm going to die a virgin. I like the thought of it. So pure.

Mom says, "I still worry about you, Daelyn. Honey." She rubs my limp hand. I feel blistering under the skin. "I wish we could talk about whatever it was that made you do what you did."

You would never understand, Kim. You think I'm normal; you wish I was.

"Then again, maybe it's best to put it behind us." She pats my hand. The blisters pop. "Just know how much we love you and how glad we are that you're here." She rests her head on mine.

It takes all my power not to disintegrate under the crush

of her need.

After a minute she lifts her head.

Huge relief.

"Your dad and I were thinking about driving up to Calgary this summer to see Aunt Beth and the gang."

I have two cousins. They're mean to me too.

"How does that sound?"

Go ahead, Kim, I think. Work up the itinerary if it'll make you happy. You're going to have to go without your nymphomaniac daughter.

She squeezes my shoulders and says, "We love you so much."

I know. I know they do, in their own helpless way.

At times like this, I'm thankful I don't feel love.

- 7 DAYS -

She's barely singing. Her voice is so low it's a whisper. During a break where the second sopranos have to rehearse a tricky section, she says, "I hope I'm not throwing you off."

I almost, almost look at her.

"I know I'm terrible. I'm only taking chorus because the other elective at this time is field hockey. Gaaaaaag." She bites on the tip of her fleshy tongue. "By the way, I'm Emily."

I hadn't noticed until now how fat she is. I mean, I noticed she was fat. Fat kids always notice other fat kids so they can compare themselves and think, I'm not that fat.

She's fat.

"Just elbow me if I should stop singing."

When I don't answer, don't move, don't acknowledge her existence, she goes, "You're Daelyn, right? Is it easier if I stand here to talk to you so you don't have to move your head?"

She's stepped over in front of me. Her white blouse isn't tucked in, the way we're supposed to wear it. Because her belly will show.

I keep my eyes on the floor. On her feet. Her thick ankles.

"If you don't mind my asking—"

"Everyone, from the coda," Mr. Hyatt says.

"Oops." She sidesteps back into place. She whispers, "What's a coda?" And giggles.

In another life, we might be friends.

Two fat girls? That would never happen.

The drizzle is gray and greasy. By the time I reach the bench, it's nuclear winter. A blur of black crosses my field of vision and I feel myself being yanked to my feet. "Come on!" he cries.

He practically drags me across the soggy lawn to his house. He steers me up the steps to the porch. "Did I forecast a rainy spring, or what?" he yells.

You watch the Weather Channel. Big woot.

The rain pours off the pitched roof.

He blows out his lungs. "Whew. You're soaked." He shakes out his hair. His spikes are slimy now, and dark roots are showing. "Come inside and dry off." He opens the door and holds it for me.

He waits.

He lets go. "Or don't."

I head back down the steps.

"Daelyn." He tugs my arm. "Don't be stupid."

I wrench away. I may be fat and ugly, but I'm not stupid. If anyone had ever gotten past my looks, they might've noticed I have a brain.

He splashes down the stairs and cuts me off. "You don't have to come in. Just wait for your mom on the porch."

A clap of thunder makes us both jump. Thunder scares

me. He edges around and sort of nudges me up the stairs. I stumble on the tread and he reaches out.

That earns him a smack with my book bag.

"Ow." He clutches his arm. "What do you have in there? Books?" A grin snakes across his face. "I like my women feisty."

He adds, "I like my arm broken."

I move to go, but he windmills his hands to block my escape. Except I'm not going anywhere. Yet.

Over my shoulder, I eye the porch layout. His hammock. A beat-up armchair and ottoman. I take a wide berth around him to the furniture, plop on the ottoman. It's rock hard.

He sticks his arm over the railing and holds out his hand, palm up. "Wet," he declares. "But fast moving. It should clear in exactly seven minutes."

If I only had a watch, I'd clock him.

"Do you mind if I sit?" He indicates the chair behind me.

I scoot back so he doesn't touch me.

He hurls himself over the arm of the chair. "Someone actually dumped this in our yard. Can you believe it? A classic Broyhill, 1958."

The chair, I guess he means. I smell his wet clothes and licorice breath.

"Ariel wouldn't let me keep it in my room. She's into sterilizing again. I told her, 'Woman, flea bites don't cause cancer.'"

I force myself to gaze out into the gray, to blur my senses. He can't really have cancer.

"She doesn't hear me. Like you. She's oblivious to my words and the sound of my voice."

I hear you. I just don't believe a word you say.

If I squint, I can see to the curb by the bench. I think I need glasses. It's been harder and harder to read. See, Kim and Chip? I'm saving you the expense of optometry.

"Hey, you're not wearing your neck doohickey."

The brace is in my bag, and my neck is killing me. I don't want to, but I take out the brace and strap it on. He reaches out to help, but I get up and go to stand at the railing. The rain's subsiding.

"D," he says in a sigh. "You're impenetrable."

You don't even know.

"What are we at? Five, six minutes?" He launches up and grabs my wrist to, like, check my watch. Idiot, I don't have a watch. I yank my arm, but he holds tight, then flips my hand over.

The skin fries where he's holding me. His fingers loosen a little. He's looking at them—the scars.

"I thought so," he says.

Could I have my hand back now, please?

"When did you do this?" He runs his thumb over the ridge of healed flesh. It sears.

I take back my arm.

"Were you scared?"

Why does he want to know that? Yeah, I was scared. After I did it, and lived.

Where is Kim? Doesn't she know I'd be on the bench, following orders?

"Man, death scares me. Did you cut both wrists at once?"

No, stupid. You have to switch hands. One at a time. Then the razor gets slippery with blood.

"Did you really *want* to die?" His voice is low, almost a whisper.

Her car splashes to the curb, saving me this lame game of twenty questions.

I log on. A lot of activity on the board.

School. Work. Broken relationships. Broken people.

It's depressing, reading about people taking drugs. Overdosing. This one person wrote about her two brothers dying a week apart, and now her lover has brain cancer. She's completing with sleeping pills and alcohol.

I think, These people. They're weak and tragic. They ask for it.

I summon Google. I key in the search line: "Hotchiss lymphona."

Google asks: Did you mean *Hodgkin's lymphoma?*

Whatever. I touch the link: <u>Lymphoma Information Network</u>

Hodgkin's lymphoma or Hodgkin's disease is a malignant (cancerous) growth of cells in the lymph system. The symptoms may include painless swelling of the lymph nodes in the neck or underarm area, fever that does not go away, night sweats, and weight loss without dieting. The disease is more common in boys than girls. About 10% to 15% of all cases of Hodgkin's are diagnosed in children 16 and under. Advances in treatment have significantly reduced the number of patients who succumb to Hodgkin's, but survival rates for relapsed patients with primary refracting Hodgkin's are poor.

Unfortunately, 1,320 people are expected to pass away from the disease this year."

I read the number. 1,320. 1,320.

Why couldn't I have a fatal disease? It'd be so much easier.

- 6 DAYS -

Kim's voice sounds softly in my ear, "Daelyn? You're going to be late." Consciousness swims from the underworld. Mushrooms and mold. Worms crawling out of my eyes. I choke on a clot of dirt and retch.

"Honey? Are you all right?"

My arms push out to shove her away. I dig myself out of my grave.

I slept hard. And dreamed. When I do sleep through the night, I have terrible dreams. This one shrink called them night terrors.

All the way to school the cemetery dream haunts me. I'm cold. Graveyards creep me out, the notion of being buried. Dead or alive.

My dream was one scene: me in a grave.

I hadn't planned on leaving a suicide note. Now I wonder if I should; let Kim and Chip know I want to be cremated.

Kim's voice echoes in my ears, "Have a good day, honey." Good day. Good day.

I sit in the chapel and shiver. I'm not talking to you, God.

Don't even ask. Santana is the first person to ask about my scars. I know people see them, because I feel their stares. They avoid me because they think I'm contagious. He even asked a decent question: Were you scared?

He admits to being scared. Which means maybe . . . he's telling the truth about his cancer? If he really is dying, I feel jealous. Why couldn't it be me? I'd be happy to trade places.

I'm on my way to econ when Emily descends. "Did you read the chapter on derived demand? I don't get it. I don't even understand the model of supply and demand. I sort of do, but maybe we could study together?"

Her desperation makes me sad. I've been there.

I have to do what I'm going to do. I speed up.

Her heavy footfalls sound behind me. "Are we late? My watch says we still have two minutes."

Don't, Emily. Please.

I practically sprint into the classroom and take a seat. It's not my usual seat by the door. As I slide in, I see her pausing in the threshold, uncertain.

Trust your gut, Emily.

She squeezes into her regular desk. Smart girl.

My mind wanders. Dirt. Ashes. I'm at lunch, eating alone. One J_Doe on the Final Forum suggested a suicide note like this:

Dear
___mother
___father
___lover

___other

There was nothing you could do to stop me because:

   ___I'd already made up my mind

   ___I have been suffering my whole life

   ___you were too slow to notice

   ___you weren't there

I offed myself because:

   ___you suck

   ___the world sucks

   ___my life sucks

   ___my job sucks

   ___my vacuum sucks

You shouldn't joke about suicide. But it was kind of funny.

The fungal, moldy taste sits in my mouth. I see Emily, eating alone too. She reminds me too much of me. Except she has kind of a bubbly personality, where mine is inert. I eat lunch in the kitchen, while the cooks are serving. Kim and Chip arranged for the cooks to blenderize my shepherd's pie and let me eat it there.

I think about Santana, and I wonder if it hurts to have cancer. He doesn't appear to be suffering. How long does it take to die?

Emily gets up and leaves. JenniferJessica trips her and I lose my appetite.

He's on the bench, elbows on knees, picking at his cuticles.

"Hey." He smiles up at me.

He seems different. Why?

He's left me room at the end. I'd decided to write him and tell him to leave me alone. Please, in a nice way, go away, I really can't deal with you. I pull out my econ spiral, which is mostly blank.

"What does this look like to you?" he says. He claws down his collar and cricks his neck toward me. "Right here."

His hand grazes a bump. I turn my head slowly to look.

"If it's another lump and I'm already on chemo . . ." He pulls up his collar and shudders. "Man." Straightening his back, he stretches his arms over his head and says, "I'm just paranoid. That never goes away."

Without even realizing it, I write, "I know."

His eyes meet mine and there's something. Understanding?

I avert my gaze.

His legs extend and he sprawls back on the bench. An arm slithers across my shoulders. Are you crazy! I scoot forward.

"I'll probably need high-dose chemo and stem cell transplantation this time. Fun and games."

He's making me feel queasy. My spiral starts to slip and I smack it onto my lap.

"Maybe I'll lose my hair again. I'm pretty hot as a skinhead." He turns and grins.

I can't stop my fluttering stomach. Am I blushing? I brush hair across my face to hide it. I start to write, "Would you please—"

"I don't want to tell Ariel about this new lump. She's already in hyper mode about the relapse. Do you think I should? I mean, there's nothing she can do. It's my war to win. She'll only cry and make both of us feel miserable and guilty that we have to get through this again, and she's not even the one who's sick." He shakes his head. "I know it's hard on her. If I don't tell her she'll kill me." He pauses. "That was supposed to be funny."

I write, "What is chemo like?"

He reads it and says, "Indescribable horror. I must be getting used to it, though, because the side effects aren't so bad this time."

I swallow and it hurts.

"If I have to, I'll do chemo to fight the beast. Whatever it takes to stay alive." He touches me and I bolt upright. The only escape is school, so I charge for the gate.

Who do I run into? JenniferJessica. A black Mercedes pulls to the curb and honks. On her way past, she looks from me to Santana. "Hey," he says.

A sneer curls her lip.

I hope he sees.

"Whassup?"

She doesn't answer him.

Santana watches as she climbs in the Mercedes and it zooms away. He widens his eyes at me. "She's a scary bitch."

He has no idea.

"Daelyn—" He snags my arm.

I pull away and slam the gate after me.

Question: *How will you be remembered?*

Subject to interpretation, again.

Not with a headstone, I can tell you that. Do *not* put me in the ground.

Here lies Daelyn Rice.

She was nice.

No, she wasn't. She was horrid.

Flush me down the toilet. Human waste.

I suppose I'll be remembered as dull. Timid.

No one ever knew me. People came. They went.

I was kind, I think. Not sympathetic, but considerate of others. I always gave up my place in line. I loaned out pencils and paper, or let people take them from me. I never reported a sexual assault.

How will you be remembered?

No one will remember—

A knock on my door startles me. Kim appears. She's different too. What's going on? She's solid and . . . glowing. I have her light brown eyes.

"You have a phone call," she says. In her hand, she holds her cell. Who would call me? Not Emily. Please.

"It's Santana."

She walks toward me with the phone. She looks at it, like she doesn't know what to do. She's not the only one. "Okay, here she is," she talks into the cell. She hands it to me.

I don't know why I take it. Or hold it to my ear.

"Daelyn, it's me. I was going to ask you something, but I chickened out. Now or never, right?"

What's he talking about?

"Do you have a pen?"

A pen? I search the top of my desk. Then think, This is dumb. Why?

He says, "Tap once for yes. Twice for no."

I glance up at Kim.

"Oh. Sorry," she says. She backs out of the room, smiling.

"The thing is, my birthday's next week. Friday, actually. It's my eighteenth. I was wondering if you'd have dinner with me."

Is he serious? Like, a date? What if he doesn't show up, or gives me the wrong address, or—

I feel the phone in my hand. I hear their voices in my head Taunting me. Teasing.

"Tap once for yes. Twice for—"

I snap the phone closed.

What would you like for dinner?

Is that all you're going to eat?

Do you want to see a movie?

What are you working on?

How are you feeling, Daelyn?

Are you fitting in at school?

How do you like your classes?

Have you made any friends?

Is your medication working?

Are you having thoughts of suicide?

Do you know we love you?

What are you writing now?

139

You know we trust you, right?

Did you take your medication?

Are you getting enough sleep?

Why don't you have more laundry?

Where's your neck brace?

Why does your bedroom seem empty?

Are you still on that computer?

Who will guide you to the light?

How will you be remembered?

Does this look like a lump to you?

Will you come to my birthday party?

Do you understand demand?

What is economics?

Have you increased your happiness quotient?

Where's your jewelry box?

Will you sing for me?

What are you reading now?

Is Santana dying?

How could a boy be lonely?

Am I throwing you off-key?

What does he see in me?

Will you be my friend?

What's that in your bag?

Where are you going, Daelyn?

What are you thinking, Daelyn?

Why are you crying, Daelyn?

I don't have to answer. Until you know the question.

- 5 DAYS -

I decide to come clean, to tell all of it. I log on to Through-the-
Light and link to *Bullied.*

"Fat camp was this place in Arizona, in the desert. It
might've been an old military base. There were supposed to be
fun activities like horseback riding and swimming and crafts.
That was in the brochure Mom gave me. Dad looked at it with
me and said it looked great; Mom said she loved going to Girl
Scout camp. That should've tipped me off. She said, 'It'll be
fantastic. You'll come back slim and healthy.'"

I admit, I was semi-excited.

"The whole time I was there, I never saw a horse. The pool
was this dried-up sinkhole, and the counselors were college
students or dropouts. They'd majored in sadism."

I figured that out fast. They'd graduated with honors from
bully boot camp.

"As soon as our parents left us, the torture began. We had
to line up for our first weigh-in. They had this industrial scale
with a huge round dial and a counselor with a bullhorn who
broadcast your name to everyone."

So humiliating.

J_Doe060787 writes: *I f*ing hate the military. They screwed me royal.*

Could you listen?

"People stripped off as much as possible. Shoes and socks. Guys took off their shirts. One girl even stripped to her bra. We had to stand in single file. Girls and guys together. There was no talking, no goofing around. Weigh-ins were no joking matter."

Not then. Not now.

"People weighed like 195, 211, 250. When my turn came, I was sweating so bad I slipped on the steps and bruised my knee. They didn't care. My name rang out all over the world, so everyone knew I was at fat camp."

Like anyone cared where I was, or who I was.

J_Doe060787 again: *I f*ing hate my boss. He rags on me for everything. I f*ing hate my job.*

Then quit, I think.

"'Get on the scale,' this counselor ordered. 'Turn around.' You had to watch the dial so you could see for yourself how disgustingly fat you were.

"176. That was my first weight. The counselor measured my height. She wrote down, 'Grossly obese.'

"It was like she'd shouted it to the world: YOU ARE GROSS.

"As I was heading off the stage, this girl who'd finished ahead of me turned and said between her teeth, 'At least I'm not as fat as you.'"

That became the camp motto. At least I'm not as fat as you.

The counselors were all fit and trim, of course. The models of perfection we would never be.

Another J_Doe pops up, but I don't read the entry. It's long, and it's about him.

"We had exercises morning, noon, and night. We had to do calisthenics. Jumping jacks and sit-ups. StairMaster. Treadmill. Before we could even have breakfast, we had to run."

My feet hurt all the time. My ankles swelled. If I sit and stare at them, even now, I can see my ankles ballooning and blisters forming on the soles of my feet. They pop and ooze.

J_Doe053175 writes: *My husband beat me. He called me every name in the book, but I stayed with him. People asked why I took his abuse. Because I loved him, that's why. Then he left me for another woman.*

That's love? To let someone beat you and be hateful to you? These people are all so . . .

Weak. Powerless to change their lives. I know the feeling. All you can do is take it. No one understands how it beats you down.

I need to stay on track here.

"Breakfast was, like, a bowl of oatmeal, watered-down orange juice, and a dry slice of toast. You ate as slow as possible because right after breakfast you had to do more exercises."

J_Doe081493 replies: *Did you lose weight?*

Someone's reading this. I want to reply, "Why? Because you'll put up with abuse as long as you get what you want?"

I don't want to discuss it at the moment. I just want to write this out.

143

"There was an obstacle course with climbing walls and rope ladders and sandpits. There were even snakes in the sand."

Not real ones. Rubber. Still, it wasn't funny. None of it was funny.

"A counselor would stand and time you and shout, 'Faster, faster. Get your big butt off the ground, girl. Move it. Look out for snakes.'"

Wasn't it enough that we had been shamed into being there?

They must've been bored, the counselors, so they used us as pawns in their sadistic little games.

I blink at the screen and see that J_Doe081493 has piped up again: *Did you say snakes?*

Forget the snakes. They were the least of it.

"We'd have to weigh in three times a day. Three. And we had to wear these black sports bras with stretchy shorts. This one counselor poked my stomach and went, 'Look at that roll of fat. Aren't you disgusted with yourself?'"

He *touched* me.

I stop for a minute to catch my breath. Drown out that roar in my head. The truth remains. I was, and am, disgusted with myself.

"On the way to the showers, we passed through the 360-degree-mirror room. A counselor on the other side would say, 'Drop your towel. Tell me what you see.'

"If you didn't answer, all the girl counselors would yell, 'Tell me what you see!'

"'Fat.'

"'What?'

"'Fat,' you'd say louder.

"'We can't hear you.'

"'FAAAT!'

"Then they'd let you out. The showers didn't have stalls, so you had to stand with two other fat, naked girls. Nobody talked."

We were mortified. Degraded.

J_Doe081493 writes: *How long were you there?*

I'm getting to that. Just let me finish.

"At night," I key, "you had to listen to these tapes. Self-help tapes. They helped convince you that you were a disgusting, worthless pig."

I can recite them in my sleep. "I am fat. I have power over my weight. If I exercise and eat right, I can lose the weight and feel good about myself."

What I heard, and still hear is, "I am fat. I have power."

My fingers are cramping. I'm on a roll, though, and I need to keep going.

An IM scrolls across the screen: *Daelyn, you've been on there for an hour. It's time to quit.*

When I'm done, Chip! Let me finish this.

"Fat camp was six weeks long."

Does that answer your question? Six weeks of hell on earth.

I'm cutting you off.

I quickly key, "10 more minutes. OK?"

I key frantically, "You got to call home every other day. I remember this one call when I talked to my mom. A counselor sat in on all the conversations. They'd listen and glare if

145

you said anything negative. Mom said, 'How are you doing?' Threatening glare from the counselor. 'Fine,' I lied. The counselor would then shove your progress report across the desk. You were supposed to say, 'So far in total I've lost 12 pounds and 5 percent of my body mass.' Because the camp guaranteed results."

They didn't guarantee you'd come out a whole person.

"I told my mom the truth. 'I put on 2 pounds.' The counselor lunged like he was going to strangle me. Go ahead, I thought. I wanted Mom to say, 'Maybe you'd better come home then.' Instead, she went, 'That's OK. It's probably muscle.'

"I had to fight so hard not to cry. Mom said, 'How are you feeling about yourself?'

"That's when I lost it. The counselor grabbed the phone from me. He told Mom some bs about what a rough day I'd had and how a small weight gain was normal and how great I was doing overall.

"When he hung up, he said, 'Your parents are paying a shitload of money to send you here. Don't disappoint them.'

"I couldn't stop crying. I was so homesick, and I hated fat camp so much. If you cried, you had to run. Crying was a sign of weakness, and they were getting paid to beat the weakness out of you."

Time's up, Daelyn.

I power down. My neck hurts and I want to close my eyes and not hear the voices.

Not see the 360-degree mirror of my life.

- 5 DAYS -

I feel lighter today. In spirit or something. It's Sunday. Day of rest. I log on and it still says 5 *days*. Yesterday was five. Today is four. What's the matter?

I log off and log on again. 5 *days*. I keep logging off and logging on, logging off and logging on. I try the PC on my desk. 5 *days*.

What's wrong? Did Chip screw something up? You can't trust machines. You can't trust people.

I know what they're doing—giving me an out. But I won't take it. I'll count the days down myself if I have to. As long as I stay, I'll always be counting the days.

Kim pops her head in. "Daelyn? Let's go to the art museum."

What? Why?

Apparently there's an exhibition of Amish quilts she's been dying to see. "I used to quilt with my mother," she says on the way. "I bet you didn't know that."

She never talks about her childhood. My grandmother died before I was born. No, I didn't know she could quilt. I bet the whole secret life she's been keeping from me explains why I'm the pathetic loser I am.

As I'm standing in the museum wondering why these quilts are on a wall instead of on someone's bed keeping them warm, Kim stumbles backward and plops on a bench. She presses her fingers into her eyelids.

I go sit with her. She's crying.

"I'm sorry," she says. "It's nothing."

Nothing. And everything.

I hate when my mom cries.

I want to put my arm around Kim, but I can't bring myself to do it. I try. I really do.

I watch as visitors file through the room. They speak in hushed voices, oohing and ahhing as they point out patterns and shapes. "The exquisite needlework," they whisper. "The handiwork." Who has time to sew a quilt by hand? I wonder. Not Kim. How long does it take, anyway? I want to ask Kim, but . . .

It's too late. She doesn't have time to teach me how to sew.

It better not be stuck on five days forever. What did Chip do?

People move on and we're alone. Kim says, "It's peaceful here." She blows her nose.

It's enormous—a vaulted ceiling, stark white walls.

It feels cold. If we could wrap up in those quilts . . .

"How are you, sweetheart?" She takes my hand in both of hers and raises it to her lips.

I feel a crack in my wall.

"Have you tried speaking? The doctor said your vocal cords should've healed some by now."

There's no reason to speak. I have nothing to say.

All the years of therapy, the doctors, the pills, the motivational tapes and books and speakers, voices, voices in my head. Empty, empty words.

"You know I'm here for you. I always will be." Kim leans into me and rests her head on my temple. My throat catches, but the weight of her skull bends my neck, and a sharp pang shoots through me. I'm glad I wore my brace.

I close my eyes. I remember this one time we went to the ocean, just Mom and me. We played on the warm beach. We built castles with moats, and I buried Mom in the sand up to her neck and she called out, "Help, help." Just kidding around. That snaps me back and forth between past and present. We played until the tide came in. Then all the memories seep up from the grave where I thought I'd buried them.

"Oh, sweetie."

Wetness on my face. Is that me? I swipe a tear away. The purging was supposed to make me feel better, not worse. I haven't even gotten to the bad part.

- 4 DAYS -

Thank God the counter restarted. Not you personally, God. Just . . . thanks.

Kim shatters my cheery mood at breakfast. "I'm sorry, Daelyn. Your father and I both have afternoon meetings we can't reschedule. Why doesn't your school give us more warning when you have partial days?"

She waits for me to answer.

Kim, that's not the question.

"Anyway, it works out fine. I took the liberty of stopping by your friend Santana's house yesterday before I went grocery shopping."

What?

"I talked to the mother. She's . . . well, never mind. You're to go over there at noon. Her shift starts at two, but Santana promised he'd stay with you."

Alone? No.

I scrape back my chair and stand. Kim grabs my wrist. "Please, Daelyn. Don't get upset."

Upset? UPSET?

The pleading in Kim's eyes . . .

I reclaim my hand from her and sit back down.

"I'm just so glad you have a friend." She smiles. And winks.

There's an earthquake inside me.

"Please," she says again. "Do this for me?"

Do what, Kim? Lead a normal life? Too late. Way too late.

"It's funny." Kim sprinkles another packet of Splenda into her coffee. "He calls her Ariel." She makes a face at Chip. "Don't you think that's odd?"

You could've asked me, Kim, at least. I would have told you no.

I can't spend time with Santana. I can't allow attachment. It's hard enough to sit by and know he has what I want, without even trying.

"Can they be trusted?" Chip glances up from the morning paper.

Can *you*? I want to scream.

"They seem fine," Kim answers. "She asked me in for a cup of chai. I didn't even know what it was. It's this spicy tea. She's very, um, earthy. The house is pristine, though. Lovely, actually. She's an artist."

I stand and leave the table.

Kim catches up with me in my room. "It's only two and a half hours, Daelyn. You can't sit on that bench for two and a half hours. And you're absolutely forbidden to walk home."

Watch me.

"I didn't tell Ariel about . . ." She pauses. "You're not being babysat, if that's what you think."

Abandoned, you mean.

"You're doing so well; going to school, making friends . . ." That gleam in her eye.

Chip shadows Kim in the hall. I grab my book bag and charge them. They both jump aside.

Out at the car, I have to wait until Kim unlocks my door. She says to me or Chip, who's still behind her, "Santana's writing a memoir, of all things. Not writing. Filming. What is he, sixteen? Seventeen?"

The lock clicks and I fling open the door. Chip presses a hand to the window. Through my fog of anger, I hear him say, "Have a good day."

Kim just guaranteed I won't.

She's still doing it, pushing me into situations I can't handle, making me cope. She knows I can't cope.

She backs out of the carport. Drizzle immediately films the window, and she flips on the windshield wipers. "I can tell he likes you." Kim smiles at me. "A lot."

It feels like a hunk of raw flesh is lodged in my throat.

Emily is absent today, so at least I don't have to deal with *that*. No one else knows I'm alive, which means they won't notice when I'm gone.

I can't help wondering how long he has. More than four days, at least.

After school, at noon, they're waiting at the gate, Santana and his mom. "Ariel, this is Daelyn. Daelyn, Ariel." Santana circles a hand between us.

"Hello," she says. Ariel clasps my hand and shakes it.

My book bag falls off my shoulder and Santana grabs it. I notice how thin his fingers are. Bony knuckles, like his knees. He takes the bag from me with his free hand, the one not holding the umbrella. I'm under siege.

Why is it raining again? I want to ask Santana. Blame him.

For the weather? That's out of anyone's control.

An arm slides around my waist and I stiffen. It's Ariel. "Santana's told me so much about you," she says, pulling me into her side, out of the rain. She has a strong grip.

What has he said?

The sick girl. The freak.

The rain spatters the clear plastic umbrella dotted with little duckies, and Santana presses in on me too. The touch of him radiates shock waves through my body.

I wonder—is it possible—is the medication working? I'm feeling things I've never felt before. I have to stop taking my pills.

I feel as if I'm hovering, my feet never touching the ground as our momentum carries us up the steps to the porch. "Welcome to Sterilization Nation." Santana shakes the umbrella over the railing.

"Oh, stop it." Ariel smacks his back. She lets go of me and my first impulse is to flee.

Santana anticipates my move. He stabs the umbrella out in front of me and I plow into it.

"Back," he says. He jabs at me until I'm at the door. Opening the door, he sweeps his arm in a low bow and goes, "Ladies?"

Ariel touches my wrist, then clenches it. Before I can

dissociate, I feel the warmth of her flesh on mine. Those pills. She pulls me into the house. They're poison.

The interior is warm, homey. It smells like cinnamon. I've only ever lived in cold, white condos.

"The sterilization procedures begin with shoes," Santana says. He steps out of his wet flip-flops on the carpet runner. Ariel removes her rubber clogs. "If you wouldn't mind," she says to me.

When I hesitate, Santana goes, "I can't convince her that there's no statistical evidence linking muddy shoes with malignancy."

"Stop it." She lightly whaps Santana's head. She's taller than he is. And larger. She's a large woman. Big-boned. Not fat. "Come to the kitchen for lunch after you've given Daelyn the tour." She pads down the long hall that runs next to a stairway leading up. On the other side is the living room, I guess. It's octagonal. A plasma TV takes up one whole wall. The chairs and couch are covered with sheets.

He raises his voice loud enough for Ariel to hear. "Take off your shoes. So you don't spread my cancer cells."

She doesn't respond.

I recoil. What if my feet stink? He's too close, making my pulse race. I take a step or two away from him, stumbling into the living room.

The intimacy of the house wraps around me. It feels like a home. My eyes stray to the living room ceiling and I almost catch my breath.

Santana says, "Yeah. She's painting the ceiling."

This is my vision—what I imagine I'll pass through on

154

my way to the light. The blue sky, the clouds, the rays of light.

"She's the reincarnation of Michelangelo—she thinks. Never question the sanity of a woman who can render you defenseless with a look." He smiles at me and my skin sizzles. I propel farther into the living room.

"It's cool, though," he says, padding in behind me, past me, his bare feet sticking on the hardwood floor. Suddenly all I see are his feet flying in the air. He's tipped over backward onto the sheeted couch. "Check it out at this angle."

Like what, on top of him?

I panic and make a beeline for the door.

"Oh, no, you don't." He's up and on me before I can escape. "I have orders from your mother to keep you here."

I wrench my wrist away from him and instinctively back into a corner.

He holds up both palms. "Sorry."

Just . . . keep your hands off me.

His eyes change. They glint mischeviously. "Don't even try to talk your way out of this, Daelyn. You are my captive now." He rubs his hands together. *"Mooahaha."*

So you think. He takes a step forward and I shove him back hard.

He stretches out his tee and looks at it. "I'll never wash this shirt."

Shut up.

A teasing smile sits on his lips.

I slow my racing heart. Okay, he's just messing with me.

"Shoes." He points to my feet. "If you don't do it, I will."

My toes curl in my shoes.

155

Santana lets out a breath. "Play the game, Daelyn. That's all you have to do."

He sounds defeated. I know the feeling.

My shoes are St. Mary–approved loafers. It's not like I'm stripping for him; I'd never do that. I slip off my shoes.

"Excellent," Santana says. "Now we indulge Ariel by pretending to enjoy the macrobiotic feast she's prepared." He scoops the air and steps aside. "After you."

Ariel says, "Not this again."

Santana repeats, "I want a dog for my birthday."

Ariel says to me, "He does this every year. He knows he's not getting a dog. You got a computer," she informs him.

Santana says, "That was a pity present."

"A what?"

"It doesn't have to be a huge, hairy dog. Or a purebred. In fact, I prefer a pound mutt."

"No!" Ariel snaps.

Santana pouts.

"You're only refusing because you think I'll die and you'll end up having to take care of my dog."

"Stop it!" She pounds the table, rattling dishes.

There's a long silence where the anger in the room is palpable. I want to go home.

Finally, Santana says, "I bet my father would get me a dog."

Ariel throws up her hands. "Oh, here we go." She places a hand on my arm, which makes me even more tense. "He keeps doing this to me," she says. "Santana doesn't have a father."

Do I arch my eyebrows?

Santana takes a bite, then garbles, "Immaculate conception."

Ariel gets up. She has a waist-long braid, graying, with frizzy bangs. Her hand touches my brace in back and I bend forward, over my bowl. She goes to the counter, lifts the pitcher, and refills my lemonade. "His father died before he was born. Even before we were married."

Santana says, "Oh, you had to add that."

"He was killed instantly in a rock slide when a boulder crushed his car." Ariel sits between us, thank goodness.

Santana downs his whole glass of lemonade.

I concentrate on picking through this stew, or whatever it is. How does she know it was instant? He might have suffered.

Instant death is difficult to achieve by one's own hand. Gunshot to the head. Explosive device.

Ariel adds, "We were getting ready for our wedding that afternoon."

What?

Santana cuts in, "Daelyn doesn't want to hear this."

Now I do.

"I'd asked Santana's father to run to the Safeway in Breckenridge to buy me some Maalox because I had an upset stomach."

Santana rolls his eyes. "Here it comes."

"Which turned out to be morning sickness."

He groans. "Please. Not while we're eating." He angles his head at me. "Your suspicions are confirmed. I am a bastard."

She grips his wrist. "You're a love child." To me she says, "I loved that man with all my heart."

Santana goes, "He's the only one who'd ever have her."

She cranks his wrist hard. "I never married. Never met anyone I'd want to marry."

"Right. Daelyn can blame my lame attempts at wooing her on the lack of a male influence in this house."

"Oh, for God's sake." Ariel fake slaps his cheek. "Apparently your wooing paid off."

Santana flushes. "Daelyn had to come. It wasn't her choice."

At least he gets that.

Now I like Ariel for making him blush. I duck my head and smile inwardly. Ariel refills my glass of lemonade again, even though I've only taken a couple of sips. Acidic liquids burn my throat.

"Santana never said why you can't talk. Did you tell me and I forgot?"

"Like I could get a word in edgewise over your incessant babble," he says.

Ariel deadpans me. "I suggest you dump him now. Unless you want a lifetime of his sassy mouth."

"And it'll be a lifetime. Give me a blob of that brownie poop." Santana holds up his plate. "Please."

You dump friends or boyfriends. Santana is neither. I don't know what he is.

While Ariel's back is turned, Santana finger gags. The lunch she made, the quinoa stew—she pronounced it "keen-wa"—was bland. It was the texture of gooey rice, and unfortunately, I found I could swallow it a few mushy kernels at a time. And fat-free, sugar-free, cocoa-free brownies would only be edible laced with arsenic.

"Were you born mute?" Ariel sets the plate in front of Santana and slides another glop of brownie goop off the spatula onto my plate. "Or were you in an accident?"

"Don't be rude, Ariel," Santana says.

"I'm not rude. I'm interested."

"Maybe it's none of your business. Maybe you should practice the fine art of butt-out-ski."

I choke down a laugh. Butt-out-ski?

Santana does a double take. "Was that a—"

"Oh, shit!" Ariel shoots out of her chair. "I need to get to work." She begins to gather plates and glasses from the table, but Santana grabs them and says, "Go. We'll clean up."

You will, I think.

Ariel hustles past the table and I want to leap up and latch on to her, beg her to stay. She skids to a stop. Twirling around, she comes back and kisses Santana's head. Pressing his cheek to her stomach, she says, "He's a pain in the ass, but I love him like a son."

Santana rolls his eyes.

"Nice to meet you, Daelyn." She smiles at me. "It's about time Santana had a girlfriend."

I choke, literally, and Santana annihilates Ariel with a glare.

Ariel pats my back until I catch my breath. Please, I silently plead with her. Don't go.

"Behave yourselves," she calls over her shoulder. "Or don't." Her laughter spills down the hall.

Santana covers his face. Then he peeks through his fingers at me and goes, "I never told her we were . . . you know."

159

I scrape back my chair. He gets up too and says, "You see the problem. Right?" His eyes shift to gaze down the hall after Ariel. He says in a flat voice, "I'm all she's got and if I don't make it this time . . ."

You'll pass through the light.

A ribbon of guilt twists my stomach. I'm all Kim and Chip have too. But the difference is, they'll be better off without me.

I think Santana's right, though, that Ariel needs him.

My parents will be sad for a while, and may even blame themselves, the way they do now. Eventually they'll come to peace with my decision. I hope they'll realize I'm finally at peace.

Santana looks at me and says, "So, what do you want to do?" He wiggles his eyebrows.

I get up, praying he won't attack from the rear, and hurry to the entryway, grab my book bag, and clench it to my chest. He follows as far as the stairway.

I walk past him back to the kitchen, sit in a chair, and remove my econ spiral and textbook.

Santana hovers in the threshold.

I open the notebook and write, I HAVE HOMEWORK. I hold it up for him to see.

He exhales a long breath. Then leaves me alone.

- 3 DAYS -

Today is a teacher in-service, and Chip draws the short straw.
"Do you want to go to a movie?" he asks me at breakfast. "Or take a drive? It's nice enough to go to the zoo."

I get up and find a notepad and pen. "I have a lot of homework. And my story for English is due this week," I write.

Chip says, "Are you going to let me read the story?"

I throw him two bones: a smile and a nod. Both lies.

As he's reading the newspaper, I tongue my pills. I'll flush them on the way to my room, the way I've done so many times before.

Two questions are waiting for me online. Did I miss yesterday's question?

Who becomes you?

What choice do you have?

It's not a question of choice.

I read the two questions again. This fear takes hold, like whoever is asking the questions has inside knowledge of me. What I'm thinking, feeling. Don't think. Do. Act.

Who becomes you? No one. No one should become me. When

I die, I don't want my body or soul inhabited. I wouldn't wish me on anyone.

I key, "No one."

Answer accepted.

What choice do you have?

I key, "Do we have a choice?"

Answer not accepted.

Okay, I was just checking to see if anyone was there.

What choice do you have?

I think about my choice. Either outcome is bleak. If I stay and live through high school, go to college, get a job, what will ever change? This blackness inside will never go away. I don't make friends; I'll always be alone. If I go, at least there's hope of peace. Chance of a new and better life on the other side.

I key, "None. Not for me."

Accepted.

I think about Santana and what choice he has. It makes me sad, so I stop thinking.

I open the Final Forum and read my last entry. It's long. Boring, though five J_Doe's have replied. Not replied, exactly. One picked up on the camp theme. J_Doe012654 wrote: *Bullies are everywhere. At school, home, work, camp. You can't get away from them.*

Wrong, I think. You can.

J_Doe011663 wrote: *I congratulate everyone here on their courage.*

Courage? I've never felt courageous in my whole entire life.

I open a new notepad and key, "Fat camp. Part 2.

"I got singled out. I don't know why. Why do people always target me? Is it because I'm short and they figure I can't fight back? They're right, I can't, but it's not because I'm vertically challenged."

That sounds pretentious. I delete "vertically challenged" and key, "small." I think, Invisible.

"I'm scared, okay? I've always been scared. Every day of my life I wake up terrified. I wonder who will make it their mission to hunt me down today. I can't WAIT to be rid of that feeling."

J_Doe033083 writes: *I have everything I need to kill myself. I have the plan, the place, the time, and the fury. I take medication that doesn't work. I know what it means to be happy, but I don't seem to want to be happy. Sigmund Freud had a theory that inside of everyone exists a "suicide impulse," which means we all desire to return to the state of perfect stillness that we experienced before birth. Do you hear the truth in that?*

Yeah, I hear the truth. But this is *my* truth.

"I wasn't the only one not losing weight fast enough, but they made me an example. . . .

"Like, if we were doing jumping jacks, my lead counselor would yell, '163! Step out!' The counselors thought it would be funny or motivating to call us by our weights. '163!' he shouted. 'Or 165 with muscle mass, ha-ha.' I had to come up and flop around in front of everyone. 'Higher!" he yelled. 'Spread those thunder thighs. Clap your hands over your head. Now count.'

"I could barely breathe and he makes me count out loud. 'Count!' he screamed.

"15. 16. 59. 69. I'd lose my place and he'd make me start

over. Everybody else got to stop at 100, but not me. I was in so much pain and my chest hurt and my boobs hurt from bouncing up and down. People were bent over trying to catch their breath and a couple of kids had to sit down, but the counselors would yank them up and make them start running. Or doing the StairMaster. I saw one girl counselor yell at this kid until she made him throw up he was crying so hard."

J_Doe012284 writes: *I hate my mother. F*ing bitch.*

"I was starving the whole time. At the morning weigh-in if you hadn't lost weight you had to run demerit distance before breakfast, then you got a smaller portion than everyone else or had to eat leftovers. A counselor would go around and say stuff like, 'Eat up, little piglets.' He'd snort and go, 'Wee, wee.'"

I hated him. I hated them all. They made me hate myself even more than I already did.

"This other male counselor would yell at us on the way out of the mess hall, 'You're losers! You're all losers.' It was supposed to be funny, like that show *The Biggest Loser.*"

But it's not funny. Not to people who've been told they're losers their whole lives and believe they will never be anything else.

164

- 2 DAYS -

On the way out of my bedroom, Chip informs me, "Your mom has to fly to Kansas City this morning, so I'll be taking you to school."

I can hear Kim upstairs, packing. Chip has folded his suit jacket over the back of the chair, and now he slips it on. Black suit and white shirt. Black-and-white-striped tie. He looks sharp. He looks like he's going to a funeral.

"Did you finish your story?"

I shake my head an inch to each side. Give it up, Chip.

Kim clomps down the stairs with her suitcase. She touches my back lightly. "I'm sorry about this," she says. "I'll be home tomorrow. Then I think this weekend we should redecorate your room. It's looking awfully bare in there. Your father won't be able to pick you up after school, so I've arranged for you to go to the Girards' again."

What? No. It took all my willpower to sit there and pretend to do homework, knowing he was close by.

"Santana said he would prepare the den of iniquity." Kim enters my field of vision and smiles at me. "What does he mean by that? Or do I want to know?"

165

He's joking. He'd better be.

She clutches her rolling luggage and kisses Chip. She makes a move to kiss me, but I jerk away. She meets my eyes, then winks. "Maybe you could get some decorating ideas at Santana's."

Mr. Hyatt claps his hands. "Girls, quiet down." He breaks off his conversation with the pianist. "All eyes up here." He pats his sternum three short clips. It's an odd gesture, like a deaf person going me, me, me.

Emily doesn't talk to me. She doesn't talk to anyone. No one talks to her.

"Does everyone have their white shirts and black skirts for next week?" Mr. Hyatt asks.

Next week is our concert. Needless to say, I will not be attending.

"Can we at least wear black leggings?" JenniferJessica asks.

"No," Mr. Hyatt says. "Hose or bare legs. Black shoes— no boots or high heels. No open toes."

"Damn." JenniferJessica always curses loud enough for everyone to hear.

"Sister Bernard has your cummerbunds. She'll be coming around during practice to try them on you."

JenniferJessica goes, "I hope you made Emily's a double wide." The wolf pack howls.

Mr. Hyatt snaps, "Taylor, up here. Now!"

Her jaw slackens. "What? I was only kidding."

Emily's back is rigid. She stares straight ahead. She's wearing the mask I know so well.

This stab of pain pierces my heart. *Who will become you?* Emily.

Not if I can help it.

Storming to the cubbies, I pull down my book bag and open it. From inside I remove my spiral and a pen. I scribble furiously, a note to Emily.

By the time I get back, Taylor's been reprimanded. She's pouting. The sister is trying on Emily's cummerbund. Emily sucks in her stomach and Sister still has to pull tight. "It's snug."

"It's fine," Emily says. She crumples the cummerbund in her fist.

The sister says to me, "Okay, dear. Raise your arms."

First, I hand the note to Emily. I watch her lips move as she reads each word. Sister Bernard repeats, "Raise your arms, please." My arms go up and the sister pulls my cummerbund around my waist. "And yours is too loose."

Emily's smiling. In my note I wrote, "She'll go to hell. They all will. If hell will even have them." She flips the note over to my P.S. on back, where I added, "Elbow me if I'm singing flat." She giggles.

The bell rings.

"If you've been fitted, you may go," Mr. Hyatt says.

Taylor stomps out.

I drape my cummerbund over Emily's shoulder. She can stitch them together, like a quilt.

He's waiting at the gate, not with his mother this time. With the rat. "Hey." He waves. He's wearing a baseball cap and he looks cool.

He's shaved and his face is smooth and soft looking. He has long black eyelashes, and I can't be feeling this way.

It's safer with the gate between us. Then Santana swings the gate in and holds it for me, so I have no choice.

I could run. Would he chase me? If I walk and keep on walking, I could make it home. It'd be good practice.

"Ariel's working, so I hope you don't have much home-work, or you can do it later. I want to show you something." He removes his cap.

My eyeballs pop. He's dyed his hair jet-black with red tips. Scratching the rat's head, he says, "You like?"

He seems taller. And different, besides the hair. He makes me feel all jiggly inside.

STOP FEELING. Stop caring.

"We'll eat real food today too." He drops Hervé into the hat, then slings them both onto his head. "I ordered pizza." He stands there, a rat tail between his eyes.

I want to cry. I don't know why. I want to be strong, like Maggie Louise. Control myself and others.

"Are you okay? You look like you had a crap day."

How does a crap day look? How does it look any different from every other day?

"Come on. I have a cure for the craps." He takes my hand.

With every ounce of courage inside me, I want to pull away. But I don't. I'm weak. We're holding hands.

I don't even remember leaving my spot and walking with him to his house. I'm losing consciousness. Damn the drugs. I should have stopped taking them earlier.

"Coke float," he says.

We're in his kitchen. My shoes are off and the rat is on the table, perched on its haunches, nibbling a Cheeto.

My hand is whole, unblemished. It's still attached to my arm. It feels contaminated, though, and I have the strongest urge to wash my hands. I can control that urge, wash them later.

Santana's busy at the counter. He sets a purple plastic cup in front of me, the same one he brought that day I was having a coughing jag. It's a faded *Pirates of the Caribbean* cup. "Whoa." He bends down to slurp the foam oozing over the rim.

The doorbell rings.

"It's Dino Delivers." Santana bounds out of the room.

He drank from my cup. What if he's contagious? Which is stupid and irrational because I'm the one who wishes she had a fatal disease. I feel bad for thinking about contamination at a time like this.

Hervé finishes his Cheeto, then scurries over to my cup and sniffs it. He rises to his haunches again, too close. I scrape back my chair. Rats, rats, rats.

Santana pops his head in. "Let's eat out here. Grab the floats."

He'd started another one on the counter—scooped ice cream into an orange *Pirates of the Caribbean* plastic cup. The liter Coke bottle sits uncapped, ready to pour.

I don't want to touch it.

I say to Hervé, in my mind, You heard him. Grab the floats.

The TV comes on and I smell the pizza. Neither dehydration nor starvation is my chosen method of completion.

I get up and go to the counter. Slowly I pour Coke over the ice cream. You have to pour slowly, dorko, to minimize foam.

"You never told me what kind of pizza you like, so I got one cheese and one supremo grande deluxe everything on it." He glances up from the floor, where he's kneeling and smiling into my eyes. This heat swells every pore of my skin. Two pizza boxes lay open on the coffee table, and my stomach gurgles. I'll miss the aroma of pizza. The stringy, chewy goodness of melted mozzarella.

I never said there wouldn't be things I'd miss. Reading. Eating.

The couch still has a sheet on it, but it's the only place to sit. Besides next to him on the floor. I shuffle between the table and couch as I set down the floats.

"Oops, hang on." He pushes to his feet and dashes past me into the hall.

I sit. My knees crunch the edge of the table.

Great. I bruise easily. Hello, camp killers? I bruise easily.

"I can't leave Hervé running loose in the kitchen." Santana rushes back in. "Last time he chewed through the blender cord and Ariel went berserk. God forbid she can't grind up her avocado and lemon-grass goo in the morning." Hervé wraps around Santana's neck.

I pull out a slice of everything. He shoves the box closer to me.

"Plus, he figured out how to push open the back screen, and I don't want him getting out. I think he'd stick around, but the foxes might find him." Santana's index finger circles

170

over the everything until it zeroes in on a slice. The biggest wedge with the most sausage.

He chomps into it and his eyes close, his long lashes curling up. "Oh, my God," he says in a garble. "Heavenly Father, we thank you for this day, this pizza, this holy hell of a meal."

I smile to myself.

We eat in silence. I chew each bite into mush, savoring the joy of pizza. It gets a little stuck in my throat. The foam has settled on my float and I drink it. It needs another dousing of Coke.

"So, I guess you're Catholic?" he goes.

Do I make a face?

"No? I thought you had to be Catholic to go to Catholic school."

You have to be damaged, I want to say.

He says, "I'm a pantheist."

A what? I set my crust back into the box and pull another slice.

"I don't like crust either," he says. "We're a match made in heaven. You do believe in heaven?"

I concentrate on eating—chewing, swallowing. Revealing no expression.

"I'll take that as a yes. What do you want to do today?" Santana reaches for another slice. "Make out? Skip the formalities?"

My eyes shift to him.

"Gotcha." He points at me.

My face flares neon red.

He doesn't seem to notice; he doesn't see me bleed. He

leans back against the couch, his head inches away. I love his black hair and red tips. I've always wanted to dye my hair, but then people would target and tease me even more.

He says, "Pantheists—at least the naturalists among us—believe God is in all things."

Really? I want to debate him. God is nowhere.

A long minute passes. The only sound is us consuming pizza. Hervé, on Santana's shoulder, gets the discarded crusts. Santana's head twists and he stares at my neck brace. "I was wondering . . ." He chews and swallows.

Leave it alone, I think.

"If you'd watch my video memoir and tell me what you think." He lowers his half-eaten slice of pizza to the box. "It's amateurish, I know that. The quality sucks." He picks off a chunk of sausage and bites into it. "I'm not a filmmaker, by any stretch of the imagination. It's not meant for prime time. More YouTube. It's just a video record for Ariel in case—" Santana expels a slow, shallow breath.

The air in the room compresses.

Hervé scrabbles off Santana's neck and jumps onto the table. He sits up, nibbling a chunk of crust. My eyes are drawn to Santana's lump. It's there, for sure. Was it that big before?

He catches me looking. "I found two more," he says. "Under my arm. I told Ariel this morning and she flipped. She's probably beating the oncologist to a pulp as we speak."

His eyes are like a telescope. I look into them and I'm transported across the universe to a world I've never been.

"Some of this is embarrassing." He brushes flour and

cornmeal off his hands and pulls a mini DVD out from under the coffee table. Like he planted it.

He scoots across the carpet to the TV. I notice a splotch of blue paint on the beige rug, and my eyes lift. She's done, or almost done. One corner of ceiling remains. I have to tilt my torso back to get a panoramic view.

It's . . . amazing. Soft, gentle curves of creamy white clouds. Subtle shards of blue and gray.

I remove my neck brace so I can scan behind me, get the full effect. It's . . . beautiful. The front curtains draw closed, cutting off my light. Santana plops down beside me and deliberately takes the neck brace from my hand.

"Wow. This thing's heavy," he says, sounding shocked. "How long have you had to wear this?"

Too long.

"Wait." He gets up, goes to a can of paintbrushes in the corner, and fishes out a flat pencil. He gives it to me. "You can write on this." He hands me a Dino's napkin, blank side up.

I write, "Play the video."

"Fine. Be that way. I assume you'll tell me when you want me to know."

Which will be never.

Santana grabs the remote and moves the brace to the other side of him. If I need it, I'll have to reach across his lap.

"I wish you could talk, because I'd like to get your thoughts on pantheism. A basic moral belief that doing harm to oneself harms us all. That we're all interconnected."

I shoot a glare at him and hold up the napkin.

"Got it. The stuff at the beginning is boring shit. It's

173

really just for Ariel. We can fast-forward through a lot of it."
He hands me the remote.

I flip it back at him.

"God." He snatches it up. "You are so—" His jaw clenches.

Insufferable? I finish for him. Impenetrable?

He thumbs the PLAY button.

Snow. Then static. On the screen and in my head.

He's sitting so close our knees accidentally knock. I don't believe in accidents. I cram myself as close to the couch arm as I can. He smells like lime and pepperoni.

I don't smell. I hunch into a rock.

"Hi." A hand with stiff fingers shoots on to the screen. "How are you? This is me, Santana Lloyd Girard the Second." The hand folds into a fist. "And this," one finger points, "is the story," two fingers, "of my life," three fingers, "so far." Four, five, six fingers. The sixth one is rubber. The hand withdraws slowly.

"Lame, I know," Santana says beside me. "I was fourteen when I started this."

That's why I don't recognize the voice. The narrator sounds like a little kid.

"I was born on April twenty-fourth, nineteen ninety-two. A day that will live in infancy." The picture of a scrawny baby is shot from overhead. "Hiya, Ma." The big hand appears with fingers wiggling in a wave. Each finger has a smiley drawn on it.

He's right. This isn't headed for Sundance.

"My father, Santana Lloyd Girard the First, could not be present at the birth of his only child, since he bit the big one in

174

a rock slide prior to the momentous occasion. The whole mind-freak element of an accident like that should've been a warning to my mother. My mother, Ariel Celestine Beatty Girard. Hi, Mom." The hand waves. Beside me, Santana groans. "It gets worse."

"Said mother testifies that the boy Santana came into this world screaming bloody murder." A blurry face fills the screen. "And I'll leave the same way." A loud screech makes my ears squinch.

Santana lowers the volume. "This sucks big-time."

The camera pans over a naked baby in a birdbath. He has flowers in his wild, curly hair. Do I grin?

"Okay, wow," Santana mutters. He aims the remote at the TV, and a jumbled mass of photos and hands and blurry lips zoom by. A boy on a bike, then a skateboard. Is that Santana? A Hacky Sack. A dog.

"Hold it," Santana says and the film freezes. "You have to see Stripe." He rewinds a bit.

This ugly dog, like a mix between a bulldog and a Dalmatian—jowls and big brown patches—sits there with its tongue lolling out the side of its mouth. Drooling and panting.

"Stripe," the narrator goes. "Sit."

The dog stands up.

"Stay."

It leaps at the camera. The picture jumps around to the sky, the bench out front, blurry grass.

Dog again.

"Speak."

The dog lifts its paw.

I glance over at Santana. He's got a dopey smile on his face.

"Roll over. Play dead."

The dog barks its head off.

Santana chuckles beside me. "I taught him that."

"Shake."

The dog rolls over, then back again. It stands up and shakes off.

I reach for my cup of float and Santana beats me to it. He hands it to me. "That was my neighbor's dog. They got him as a pup, then left him alone all day while they went to work. Ariel won't let me have a dog because they shed. That's her rationale, anyway. God, I want a dog so bad—"

The camera zooms in on a bunch of papers that are spread across the carpet.

"Here it comes." Santana leans forward. "This is my lymphangiogram. My chest X-ray, CT scan, PET scan, and gallium scan."

There are charts and graphs and reports on the floor.

"My first biopsy results." The camera pans close.

I squint but can't read the type.

"Diagnosis: Hodgkin's disease." Santana's face fills the screen, teeth bared. He sings the first two bars of Beethoven's Fifth. "Bah-bah-bah-*bum*. Bah-bah-bah-*bum*."

The picture goes off. Then on.

The door to a room opens. Santana makes creaking sound effects on the film. A man in scrubs smiles for the camera, and the frame tilts. It does a one-eighty.

"October twenty-nine, two thousand seven. Santana

begins chemotherapy." The camera pans to a woman. Is that Ariel? She looks way younger.

Next to me, Santana breathes. His breath is warm and moist. Why does it feel like he's breathing right on me?

Someone else is filming now because Santana is in a chair, like a dentist's chair, getting an IV stuck in his arm. I shudder. I hate needles.

He winces too. Dramatically on screen, he turns his head and covers his eyes with the back of his hand. "Bloody hell."

"We can skip a bunch of this," Santana says. He sets down his float and fast-forwards. There are stretches of Ariel talking fast and making faces, posing for the camera like a model, cooking, painting on a canvas, putting on makeup. Santana skateboarding, doing chin-ups in a closet, his hair long and curly. Santana sprawled on the bench, reading.

The film stops. "That bench is made out of the rock that killed my father. Ariel had it brought down from the mountain and carved. Kind of morbid, but every year on my birthday we sit there and she tells me about him. I sort of feel like I know him."

I can't help looking at Santana. His expression is somber.

My stomach wrenches. That's their bench. I've been invading his personal space.

"Hey," Santana shifts his torso to face me, "did you realize that bench, our bench as I've come to think of it, sits directly underneath an anise magnolia tree? Anise smells like licorice. Magnolia—Maggie Louise?" He waggles a finger at me. "I'm telling you, Daelyn. Interconnections."

When I make a face, he says, "You're right. Excessive commentary."

The film continues. Santana sleeping, his hair messy.

"Wait." He stops the film and rewinds.

Santana sleeping. "Here he is," a woman whispers. "My sweet, perfect, brilliant baby boy."

In my peripheral vision, Santana's Adam's apple bobs. Or is that the lump?

"I forgot she took that," he says.

The film rolls. His younger voice says, "Hair today. Gone tomorrow."

Santana waves an electric shaver across the screen. He flicks it on and it buzzes. He aims the teeth toward his head, where his hair is already patchy in places, and when the shaver hits his head, he grimaces. He squeezes his eyes shut and clenches his teeth. The razor carves a naked swath over his scalp. "Owwww."

I can't watch this. My gaze drops to the cheese on the other pizza, which is congealing. Plus, Hervé's walking on it. We demolished the everything. Hervé missed a crust, so I flip it at him with the pencil.

"Mom, don't."

I glance over. Santana's eyes are glued to the screen.

He's on the couch, this couch I guess, without the sheet. It's blue-and-gold brocade. Santana's sleeping, or pretending to. He lifts his arm and shields his face.

"You wanted me to record everything at the same time every day. Smile," Ariel says.

Under his arm, on the couch, Santana forces a weak smile.

In the next shot, he's hurling in the toilet.

My stomach churns.

"Sorry." Before Santana can fast-forward, I see him resting his forehead on the toilet rim. I think, This is why he was homeschooled.

In fast-forward, Santana moaning.

Sleeping.

Clutching his stomach.

Lying on the couch, curled into a fetal position.

Santana sitting on the bench. Staring into the camera.

He reaches over and takes my hand. For real.

Wide eyes. Staring at the lens.

Ariel's voice: "I can't do this anymore."

The film ends.

Do I squeeze his hand?

Santana's other hand raises and brushes my chin. He moves my head around slowly to face him. Then he scoots over fast, closing in. His lips touch mine. The shock of it makes me tense, but his lips are soft. He presses a little harder, too hard, pushing me back with nowhere to go and I'm trapped and it's . . .

Black. Blinding white light. Santana holding me down suffocating me with his mouth—

My fingers tighten around the pencil and I stab him in the arm. The lead is dull and I stab and stab until he cries out, "Ow." He goes, "What the hell?" and rolls off me.

The doorbell rings.

Kim is here to save me at last. At *last*.

I lie in bed, the cover up to my chin, shivering. How could he? How could he betray our trust? I TRUSTED him. For the first time ever. He was my . . .

What?

Friend? I don't even know the meaning of the word.

My eyes close and the room spins, a vortex. I'm back in the boys' bathroom again; Toomey's kissing me, lifting up my skirt, pulling down my underwear. I try to scream, but no sound comes out—

My eyes fly open.

Why? Why did I let him do that to me?

All of them. The teasers and bullies and perverts. Yes, perverts.

I throw back the covers and bounce out of bed, snag the laptop and return, jamming against the headboard.

I press the power button.

My brain says Through-the-Light, but my hand takes me to IM.

He's there. He's been on a while because he's already written:

herveh0tsu: D, talk to me

herveh0tsu: Talk to me

herveh0tsu: Talk to me

herveh0tsu: I'm not going away

Why? If he doesn't see how sick I am by now . . . What is he, dense?

herveh0tsu: D, you're on. Talk to me.

I wish I was invisible to him, to everyone.

herveh0tsu: TALK TO ME DAMMIT

I key, "no. and don't call me D. it's daelyn."

herveh0tsu: Got it. What happened? Why'd you freak out? I thought we were getting somewhere.

"where?"

herveh0tsu: hell, I don't know. 1st? 2nd?

Third? Fourth grade?

"i can't"

There's a pause.

herveh0tsu: Ok. How was I supposed to know? You never call. You never write.

If I could laugh . . . He makes me feel fluid inside. I'm terrified of the feeling.

I key, "what do u want from me?"

herveh0tsu: Your hot bod? What else? I'm an animal.

No, you're not.

herveh0tsu: I like you. What I know of you.

"which is 0"

herveh0tsu: Exactly. So we're back to your hot bod.

I should be offended. Instead, I feel grateful. I'm so desperate.

herveh0tsu: Is it a crime for a guy to like a girl?

I key, "in that way, yeah"

herveh0tsu: What way?

Never mind, I think. I don't know.

herveh0tsu: Come on. Give a dying man his last wish.

I punch the OFF button. That is so not fair.

Tears well from somewhere inside me and overflow my eyelids. They stream down my cheeks and into my open mouth; they salt my wounds. I close my burning eyes and fight to keep the emotion from drowning me.

There's a knock on my door.

I press the laptop power ON and hunch over the keyboard.

Chip says, "I'm going to bed now. You should too."

My hair shields my face.

He eases the door almost closed. "G'night, sweetheart. Sleep tight."

I hold my breath to keep from losing it.

Santana's still on, messaging away.

herveh0tsu: Don't go, daelyn

herveh0tsu: DAELYN!!!

herveh0tsu: God. I'm sorry. I'm an ass

herveh0tsu: a

herveh0tsu: s

herveh0tsu: s

herveh0tsu: hole

herveh0tsu: I keep using it as an excuse. I wasn't trying to pressure you into anything you didn't want to do. Guilt you into it maybe by making you watch my vid.

A pause. An interminable wait.

herveh0tsu: daelyn?

I key, "an excuse for what?"

herveh0tsu: Being an asshole. Getting my way.

I key, "sorry excuse"

herveh0tsu: no shit

Another wait. I should say something. I don't know how to talk to a boy.

herveh0tsu: Give me something. Anything. You know my whole life story.

Do I? Can you know a person from their video memoir?

herveh0tsu: Tell me about the neck brace

Why? I sit and stare at the screen. Why that? The brace is

on the rocking chair where I flung it when I staggered in and crashed to bleed out internally.

hervehOtsu: You don't have to. You don't have to do anything. I'll leave you alone from now on.

He signs off.

I key quickly, "i drank ammonia and bleach so i could die. r u happy now?"

- 1 DAY -

"A boy died at camp. Police came, an ambulance, a fire truck. Our parents got called to come and pick us up. I heard someone say the kid had a heart attack from too much physical exertion. As they were carting him off on a gurney, all I could think was, I wish that was me."

J_Doe051676 writes: *I just wanted everyone to know this will be my last post before I leave this life. I've been planning my suicide for three and a half years, making sure everything is in order, and finally I can act on those plans. In a couple of hours I will be free. Already I'm relaxed and less stressed. I don't know any of you, but I felt it was necessary to let somebody know of my end. I'm finally going to my rapture.*

Does he have to make a big announcement?

These people are pathetic.

I switch over to DOD and see J_Doe051676 on the list.

At least he wasn't lying.

The weariness of it all is seeping in again. I power down and shut my eyes. The purging worked. I feel better, released from my bondage.

A haunting image swirls into focus. It's Santana. That last frame of film. The swollen cheeks and sunken eyes.

Stinging behind my eyelids, but it feels right.

Life is so unfair.

The last question was the one I'd been asking all my life. *Why are you here?*

That's the question.

Why *am* I here? What's my purpose?

"Daelyn, are you up?" Chip calls. He's right outside my door and he reaches around to knock. "You dressed?" He gives me a minute to collect myself before poking his head in.

"Oh. Good. You're not on the computer."

I throw the last book into my book bag. *Desire in the Marsh.* It's hard to believe I'm almost to the end. I'll miss Maggie Louise.

She's my friend, my idol.

How stupid. A character in a book can't be your idol. They aren't real or alive. They never had to act courageously in the face of real adversity or fear. These books are terrible. I don't know why I gobbled them up in middle school. I'll never know romance or adventure or love.

This is the last book in the series and I already know how it ends, but I made a commitment to read the books again, and the goal must be completed. I have to accomplish something, to prove to myself—

What? That the only friends I've ever had are imaginary? The goal, the goal. I have to reach the end. If I read in the chapel and during classes, at lunch, and after school, I can finish.

Chip greets me in the kitchen with my cereal and pills. I tongue the pills and when he turns around, spit them into my hand. "Your mother called while you were in the shower. She said this audit is taking longer than she expected and she won't be home until late Friday."

Friday?

My heart pounds. Blood courses through my veins and I feel hot, then cold. I won't see my mother again.

Chip is chatty on the way to school, talking about this time he and Mom drove to Carlsbad Caverns. I'm in shock. I'll never see my mother again. "We were taking a second honeymoon, hitting all the hot spots and the tourist traps from here to Las Vegas." I feel catatonic. "The car broke down in Death Valley and we had to thumb a ride. A couple of college kids picked us up. They were on their way to Vegas to get hitched." Chip smiles at me. "On a whim, your mom and I decided to renew our vows in Vegas." He shakes his head like the memory just jarred loose. "If you elope, I highly recommend the Viva Las Vegas Wedding Chapel." He chuckles. "I believe you were conceived in the Blue Hawaii room."

A wave of nausea makes me lurch.

"Are you okay?" Chip reaches across and touches my arm. "Do I need to stop?"

The word "no" forms on my lips as I clutch my stomach. What was the last thing I said to her?

Chip goes, "We were told that we couldn't have children, so you were a miracle baby. I want you to grow up, get married, and have lots of kids. Grandkids for me and your mom to spoil. You have so much to look forward to in life, Daelyn."

* * *

Emily is waiting for me at the chapel. "Hi." She smiles and waves.

I slow. If I run, she'll never catch me.

I don't know what to do. I guess I started this.

"Did you study for the econ test today?" She follows me into the nave.

We have a test? I guess I was sort of distracted.

"I always get so nervous before a big test." She waits for me to choose a pew. I head for the middle section, left aisle, clear at the end by the confessional, then hesitate. These pews are narrow. There's no one in the chapel. We could sit anywhere. I walk up to the front where you don't have to squeeze in.

I let her go first. She smiles as she passes. I mean, this huge smile that turns her cheeks pink and her eyes twinkly.

She rolls out the kneeler from under the pew, kneels, makes the sign of the cross, and folds her hands.

I don't pray. I just like the peace.

I watch Emily, the seams around the arms of her white blouse pulling taut. She rests her forehead on her folded hands, and I think, She's going to need her faith.

Out the open window, I see him. Taylor, aka Jennifer Jessica, has called him over to the fence. She's tossing back her hair and he's krumping in place. Is she laughing, enjoying it? My heart hurts. I have no reason to feel jealous. I can't give Santana what he wants. A nun bustles over and shoos him away and he backs up, waves, and krumps off. Taylor's groupies swarm around her and howl at something she says. She peers over her shoulder. They're making fun of him. She's mocking him. I want to get up and—

Emily crosses herself again and sits back.

Don't make fun of him! I scream inside. He's dying.

In a whisper, Emily says, "Thanks for your note. I needed that."

I tender a grim smile.

"I thought this year would be different, you know? High school and all. I thought people might be more mature, or nicer, at least."

Surprise, Emily. People don't change. There are two kinds of people in the world: winners and losers.

Black and white. I don't know where gray fits in, or if you can even live in the shade.

"Does that neck cast hurt?" She studies it, tilting her head. "It reminds me of those African women who wear brass rings around their neck," she says, "and keep adding rings until their necks are stretched like a giraffe's. I read if they take off the rings, their necks snap and they die of asphyxiation."

The Padaung women of Thailand. I saw it on the Discovery Channel. They wear the brass rings to promote tourism to their villages. The rings weaken the neck muscles, so if the women remove the rings, their necks can't support the weight of their heads.

Emily says, "Supposedly, the neck rings symbolize the beauty ideal." She sticks out her fleshy tongue. "Gag."

But you'd sell your soul for it, wouldn't you? For one day of feeling beautiful.

"Okay, I'll zip it." Emily yanks an invisible zipper across her lips.

I like her. She seems to be at peace with herself. I think Emily has courage.

We sit in silence, eyes trained on the altar. The cross. What did Jesus die for, anyway? "I know I talk too much," Emily says. "It's just, I don't have a lot of people to talk to. Not a lot of people are worth my time."

I look at her. She adds, "When you showed up for chorus, I knew right away you were different. In a good way," she adds quickly.

What did she see in me? What does she see that I don't? She smiles again.

No, Emily, I think. Don't choose me. I'm not worth your time.

This is my fault. Mine. Making her think I'd be here for her.

Tearing the Velcro straps, I remove my neck brace from the front. It forms a tube and I hand it to her. More like shove it. Take it, Emily. Keep it as a token.

Because tomorrow when I go, I want you to believe friends are possible.

Emily balances the brace on her lap. She examines it, peers down the center. "It's heavy," she breathes.

Unbearably.

She looks at me. "Is your neck going to snap?"

I stick out my tongue and let my head fall back.

Emily giggles. She covers her mouth, eyes darting over our shoulders like it's a sin to laugh in church.

"Can I try it on?"

That wasn't the plan.

I don't know what the plan was. It's all I had to give.

She straps herself in. "Miracle of miracles. It fits."

I have to smile at that.

"How do I look?" She twists her whole upper body toward me.

Like a Padaung princess, I think.

The bell rings and Emily rips off the brace. I stand with my book bag and she grabs hers. She tries to return the brace, but I mime, Keep it.

"Really?"

I won't need it anymore. On second thought, throw it away.

We're almost to the classroom when Emily says, "My mom is sending me to fat camp this summer. Oh joy."

I stop dead, my book bag thunking to the floor. I snag Emily's left arm and reach across to take her right. My mouth opens and my tongue presses against the top of my palate and the word opens my throat. It takes will and rage to force sound from my scarred and melted vocal cords, but I do it. I say, "No.

"Don't.

"Go."

Emily's jaw drops. My hands clench her hard and I'm shaking. Shaking her. She nods as if she hears. She's listening.

Questions. They repeat in my head.

How will you get to the light?

Drowning. I'll bloat myself.

190

Bloater. Fatso. I never defended myself. Not once. I never said, "Excuse me? What gives you the right to insult and demean me?"

I let them steal my dignity.

Who will see you through the darkness?

Me. I'll find my way.

The darkness is a given. The darkness is life.

In that bathroom, with those boys. It changed me; made me believe in evil.

I could find my way out of that bathroom. I did. I freed myself by crawling and groping in the darkness.

That took courage. To walk out and face my class.

I should've told Kim. Chip. Anyone who'd listen. Those boys got away with violating me. In all the years of therapy, I never once spoke of that incident. Maybe if I'd named names, I'd have saved someone else from the same fate.

But I'm no hero. I had to keep my dirty little secret.

The worst sin I committed was holding it in; letting the secret blacken me.

What awaits you?

Eternal peace. Serenity.

The light on the other side.

What awaits me is unknown. The only certainty is that life is an eternal hell.

I'm scared. What will tomorrow bring?

It has to be better than today. It *has* to.

How will you be remembered?

As a loner and a loser.

Kim and Chip will be the only ones who remember me for

very long. I hope they remember the good stuff, when I was a baby, a toddler, when they still had hopes and dreams for their little girl, their miracle child. In truth, they were good to me. They were only doing what they knew how to do; what they thought was best.

I do love them.

I just hate the world they brought me into. I'll be remembered as a fat, frightened, weak, stupid kid. Too scared to stand up for myself.

Why?

Because they had power. They had numbers.

If we'd found each other, though, the tormented, the weak and powerless, we could've banded together. What made me weak was the sense that I was alone. But maybe I wasn't alone. All the people on Through-the-Light, where were they? Living in the dark spaces, the gray place. If we could've found each other sooner, would it have changed the outcome?

I don't know. What I know is you can't go back. You can't press delete and re-key your life.

How are they remembered, the ones who gave in to the darkness?

As losers, or winners?

Who becomes you?

Not Emily. She's strong. She's reaching out. To the wrong person, but she'll find others. She has to.

What will I become? Because I won't be me any longer.

That will be a relief. I don't want to be the helpless person I've always been.

What choice do you have?

NONE.

Okay, I know I have a choice. God gave me free will. I'm not talking to you, God. Take the pain with me or leave it behind. That's my choice.

Why are you here?

A body rams me and a voice says, "Watch where you're going."

Where am I going? I'm in a long, narrow hall, walking. There are people everywhere, talking and laughing.

It's school. The day is over. Where have I been?

I have to pee, and I can't wait a few minutes.

The restroom is around the corner, so I veer in for a pit stop. Santana appears in my head. How does he do it? Live. With the fear of death every day. I don't fear death as much as I fear the thought of living.

I think, He won't be waiting on the bench. He knows now I have nothing to offer. Pantheism means counting on other people to keep you alive, and in this life, I don't count.

I hear the bathroom door open and close. A rush of cold air on my legs makes me shiver.

Silence, but I know someone is here. My hand is unsteady as I go to wipe, and a drop of hot pee wets my finger. I thrust that hand away from me, stand up, and flush.

She's at the sink when I emerge. We don't speak.

I move toward the right sink and she blocks me. I edge to the left one and she blocks it too.

I have to wash. I HAVE to. I head for the exit, but Taylor's anticipated my move. She lifts both arms to the side, pressing against the tiled doorway. I need to get out that door.

"I saw you with fat Emily in the chapel," she says.

Please let me through.

"The fatty and the freak. How special."

My eyes raise to meet hers. Let. Me. Out.

She plants her feet and scans me up and down. "Funny how rumors get started." An evil smirk curls the ends of her lips.

My gaze shifts past her mocking face to the door, to freedom.

"I saw what you did."

When? What is she talking about?

Taylor purses her lips and makes a kissing sound.

She disgusts me.

The sinks are unguarded, so I rush over and wrench on the water. A sigh of relief escapes my mouth as I cleanse. Rinse. Scrape.

What am I scraping away? The filth. The memories.

"I bet your *boy*friend would be interested to hear about your *girl*friend."

When I glance up into the mirror, Taylor's behind me. She watches me scrub one hand, then the other. She goes, "You are so freaking weird." Then for no reason, she kicks me in the leg.

I whirl and kick her back. Hard.

She looks . . . shocked. "Ow," she says. "Why did you do that?" Her eyes pool. Then they slit and she looks mean.

I stumble back out of her reach.

She shoulders her bag and snarls between her teeth, "Watch your back. Freak." She rushes out the door.

Under my breath, in a raspy whisper, I say, "You watch yours."

The bench is empty. I knew it would be. Why he ever made contact in the first place . . .

I'm still trembling from the confrontation with Taylor as I fish through my bag for my book. Calm yourself, Daelyn. She can't hurt you. You're almost at the end. *Page 294. Maggie Louise brushed her auburn mane until it glistened. Charles would be here any minute and she'd tell him the news. Her mother once told her, "My darling, you've inherited your beauty from your father's side of the family." The high, chiseled cheekbones, the long, lean frame. But Magnolia's constitution? Her determination? That was her mother's gift to her.*

I'll never see my mother again. She was powerless. We all are sometimes. What did I expect her to do? Save me when I couldn't even save myself? I have the most urgent need to hug my mom, to tell her I'm sorry. To sit with her in the rocking chair and hear her sing to me.

"You must follow your heart's desire, for it will lead you to your destiny." Her mother's wise words resounded in Maggie Louise's head. She felt the child within, the baby who would only ever know love and happiness in life. Yes, she'd found her heart's desire. In Charles.

He flops down and I about jump out of my skin. He sticks out his bony, hairy legs. He has on those camo shorts that tie at the knees. They're not tied; the strings dangle. A sleeveless white tee. His hair is messy, like he just got out of bed.

195

Why is he here?

"I saw your last message," he says quietly.

My heart races. How? He wasn't supposed to.

He shakes his head. "I can't believe you."

Because then you would have to despise me, I think. You already do.

He twists his head to take me in. To drill into the side of my face. I feel his eyes penetrating my shield, and my heart explodes. He says, "I sort of figured out it was self-inflicted. Knowing you."

I don't even know me. How could he?

"I ran through all the possibilities. One," he holds up a finger, "you slit your throat. Unless you had a really sharp serrated knife or a scalpel, you'd have to saw pretty hard." He blinks. "Like, yeowch."

My breathing is rough and ragged. I can't swallow.

"Two," a second finger, "you hanged yourself. I was sure that was it, although the loss of speech didn't fit. Unless you really were mute, or choosing not to speak."

People who hang themselves empty their bowels. Leaving waste behind is not an option.

"Three was not even on my list." He lowers his hand to clutch the bench. "Ammonia and bleach." He shakes his head again. "Daelyn, that's harsh. Did it burn up your esophagus all the way down? Soak into your vocal cords? I bet your stomach lining did the happy dance on that one."

I close my eyes. Can't he see I'm not worth his time?

"If you'd asked me I would've told you, drink paint thinner. Or gasoline. Petroleum products wreak havoc on the human body."

Tears rim my eyelids.

"It's okay," he says softly.

Involuntarily, I hiccup.

He snakes an arm around behind me, curling his fingers over my shoulder. "Everyone hurts sometimes."

A gulp escapes.

"There's no shame in that." He scoots a little closer. He breathes in my hair and I cry out loud.

Santana presses my head to his chest. I'm heaving, I'm sobbing so hard.

"We all get better too, you know. I heal you. You heal me. So sayeth Santana Lloyd Girard the Second, renowned lady-killer."

That makes me cry louder.

He rests his head on mine and lets me cry it out. I think I'll drown in my own self-pity.

"Listen," he says after a while. "You never answered my question."

I sniffle and look up at him, teary-eyed. "What question?"

He gasps. "She speaks!" His eyes narrow and he waggles a finger in front of my face. "If you've been holding out on me all this time . . ." I want to bite off that finger, but instead I just wrench it down.

"Hey. You're strong." He takes my hand and won't let go. "If I don't die of Hodgkin's, the lead poisoning will kill me." He shows me on his other arm the bruise where I stabbed him. It didn't even pierce the skin. He's smart enough to know the lead in pencils is graphite. "And you're mean."

"No, I'm not." I was only defending myself.

"No. You're not. Not like some people we know." He holds my eyes and I can't look away. "So, the question," he says.

My throat is raw, dry. "What. Question?" It hurts to talk.

"About having dinner with me on my birthday."

My brain is a mass of snarling wires. Nothing computes.

He adds, "If you're around tomorrow, that is. If you don't have plans, like drinking toxic waste or running with scissors, I would really, really like to share my birthday with you."

I blink at him. "Me?" I whisper.

"Oh please." He nudges my knee, like, you have to ask? His eyes, his dark blue, deeply intelligent eyes that span the universe go serious on me. Deadly serious when he says, "You can answer that question for yourself."

198

– DAY OF DETERMINATION –

I log on and the final question appears:

Delete account? Yes No

I touch *Yes.*

Confirm? Yes No

I touch *Yes.*

My room is cleared. My head is cleared. Earlier, around dawn, I took out the last load of trash. I look around and see what's left. Nothing.

There is no more Daelyn Rice.

As I was.

As I am.

Or will become.

I'm a blank slate.

What choice do you have?

Begin or end.

Complete myself.

Out the window, the man and dog appear. Man throws the Frisbee and Dog chases it. But instead of retrieving, Dog sits. He drops the Frisbee. He makes the man come to him.

I smile to myself. Game over. Dog wins.

I wish for Santana to have a dog.

His invitation lingers. So does my question. Why me? I don't know the answer. When I look at myself in the mirror, all I see is a starving, stunted bird who never grew wings and lost all reason to sing.

Chip calls, "Whenever you're ready to leave, honey."

I stick the Mini Me into my book bag and shut the door behind me. It's time. With determination and purpose, I head into the light.

BY

THE

TIME

YOU

READ

THIS,

I'LL

BE

DEAD

———————————

DISCUSSION GUIDE AND RESOURCE LIST

PREPARED BY C. J. BOTT

About the Guide

By the Time You Read This, I'll Be Dead is not a book that calls for formulaic questions, study guides, or vocabulary lists. The power of this book grows with the questions the reader asks him/herself. Questions that we don't want to ask because the answers may be too disturbing. This is a book that challenges the reader not only to ask those questions, but also to look for the answers.

About the Book

Daelyn has been the target of bullying for many years, and the bruises from it continue to hurt her. Unable to speak due to a failed suicide attempt, Daelyn is locked into an isolation of silence that she welcomes and protects. She wants to escape school, her parents, her life. . . . Previous suicide attempts have been failures, but now, with the structured help of Through-the-Light.com, an Internet suicide site, Daelyn knows she won't fail again.

Discussion Prompts

1. Daelyn's last suicide attempt injured her esophagus and vocal cords. She can't talk to others, and at school some students think she is mute. Daelyn and her silence form a relationship.

- How does her silence insulate her?
- Does the silence keep her a prisoner?
- By the end of the book, the reader knows Daelyn can talk if she wants to. Why does she choose to speak?
- How does the author benefit from having a silent main character?
- List the advantages and disadvantages of Daelyn's silence.

2. *The worst is waking up in the hospital. Your parents are there, crying. Or your mother is yelling at the doctors and nurses. You come back wrecked. You ruin everyone's day.*

It won't happen again.
I promise. (p. 29)

- What is she promising?
- Does Daelyn's perception about how her death will affect her parents differ from the likely reality?
- Daelyn sees her parents' anger, but not their relief that she's alive. Expand on this idea.
- Daelyn is doing everything she can to make this time the last time. She has become a methodical planner. Explain her thinking.

3. Sometimes people who are broken find other people who are broken.

- Why might that be?
- How does it happen in this book?
- Can they help each other back to wholeness?

4. *Secrets. I can't take them with me. If I do, when I go, when I arrive at my final destination, I'll be . . . impure. I have no choice but to trust that they're safe here. (p. 72)*

- There is a saying, *Secrets keep us sick*. How does this fit Daelyn?

5. *By the time I was ten I already knew my destiny. By middle school I had a plan for escape, for control. There's always a way out. All you have to do is take it. (p. 113)*

- Explain how Daelyn sees "a plan of escape" as a plan "for control."
- In one sense, Daelyn seems to be surrendering, but in another she seems to have become determined. Explain how she does both.

6. Why does Daelyn sign up for choir?
   Why does the teacher go along with it so completely?

7. *Girls scare me more than boys. Boys are cruel. Girls are mean.* (p. 118)

   • Why would girls scare Daelyn more than boys?

8. *She squeezes my shoulders and says, "We love you so much."*
   I know, I know they do, in their own helpless way.
   At times like this, I'm thankful I don't feel love. (p. 126)

   • What would change for Daelyn if she did feel love?

9. *His eyes shift to gaze down the hall after Ariel. He says in a flat voice,*
   "I'm all she's got and if I don't make it this time . . ."
   You'll pass through the light.
   A ribbon of guilt twists my stomach. I'm all Kim and Chip have too.
   But the difference is, they'll be better off without me. (p. 160)

   • Daelyn and Santana are both concerned about their parents,
     but how are their concerns different?

10. Santana says: *"If I have to, I'll do chemo to fight the beast. Whatever*
    it takes to stay alive." (p. 137)

    Daelyn and Santana are each in a life-death conflict.

    • How are they different? How are they alike?

11. Why does Santana want a relationship with Daelyn?

12. *"I'm scared, okay? I've always been scared. Every day of my life I wake up terrified. I wonder who will make it their mission to hunt me down today. I can't WAIT to be rid of that feeling."* (p. 163)

- How does this quote define bullycide?
- Is it realistic to believe some people can feel this way?

13. *"I wish you could talk because I'd like to get your thoughts on pantheism. A basic moral belief that doing harm to oneself harms us all. That we're all interconnected."* (p. 173)

- Who else will be hurt if Daelyn harms herself?
- Do you believe in pantheism?

14. *Santana presses my head to his chest. I'm heaving, I'm sobbing so hard.*

"We all get better too, you know. I heal you. You heal me. So sayeth Santana Lloyd Girard the Second, renowned lady-killer."

That makes me cry louder.

He rests his head on mine and lets me cry it out. I think I'll drown in my own self-pity. (p. 197)

- Because of Santana, Daelyn is no longer alone. Has his friendship come too late?

15. *"If you're around tomorrow, that is. If you don't have plans, like drinking toxic waste or running with scissors, I would really, really like to share my birthday with you."* (p. 198)

- Why is this such a significant request?
- Do you think Daelyn doubts his sincerity? Why and why not?

16. Through-the-Light.com, a suicide board, helps Daelyn plan her suicide.

- Is this ethical?
- Is it freedom of speech?
- If it hadn't existed, would Daelyn have stopped trying to kill herself?

17. In this book, bad things happen to Daelyn.

- Is one of her attackers more guilty than another?
- Do you think any of the people who harass Daelyn want her to kill herself?

18. *Bullycide. I know that word well. Suicide as an escape from bullying.*

- Before reading this book, had you ever heard of bullycide?
- Do you think it happens a lot?

19. On the Day of Determination, Daelyn logs on and answers the final questions; she checks that she has not left anything from her past behind; she looks out the window and sees a man and his dog, and she wishes for Santana to have a dog; then she decides to complete herself. The last line is, *With determination and purpose, I head into the light.*

- What do you believe happens on that day?

Bullying

In a recent survey, 70% of all students said they feel affected by bullying. That's nearly three out of four people in any school. That's approximately 25,000,000 young people in the United States alone. The enormity of the problem is unimaginable. But not irreversible.

According to current research, the accepted definition for bullying is as follows:

- The behavior is repeated over time.
- The aggressor intends to do harm, if only to embarrass.
- An imbalance of power exists between the aggressor and the target.

There isn't an established profile of a bully or a target. Anyone can be a bully or a target. If you think someone is bullying you, use the above definition to decide if it is bullying. If your behavior upsets someone, again, check the above definition to decide if your actions make you a bully. What you believe is teasing or fooling around may really be bullying. The effect on the other person is the defining factor.

Given the above definition, brainstorm bullying behaviors you have seen on television, in the news, and in school. Group them into different types of bullying—e.g., name-calling, homophobia, body image, etc.

Name-calling is the first form of bullying most of us experience. Make a list of the hurtful words young children use to name-call.

Then make a list of names in elementary school, middle school, and high school. How do the names change? Where and when are those names most often heard in schools?

Discuss the three roles in most bullying events—the bully, the target, and the bystander/witness. Set up some bullying scenarios and get volunteers to play the bully, the target, and several witnesses or bystanders. After the role play, have each person share how he or she thinks their character feels. Create at least one role play involving a teacher as either the bully or the witness.

Brainstorm some healthy and helpful ways bystanders can react. Be sure simple behaviors are included, such as smiling at the target in the hallway, walking with the target to a class, inviting a new student or an alienated student to your lunch table.

Research shows that 70-80 percent of adults at schools do nothing after witnessing a bullying event, while others are unaware of it happening. Brainstorm ways teachers and other staff can respond to a bullying event. Why don't kids who are bullied tell adults?

Play detective. Get a map of the school, including outside areas—buses, playgrounds, sporting events, etc. Carry it with you through the day and record any bullying events you see with tally marks. Share your observations in class. Why does bullying happen in these areas?

Electronic aggression is any kind of aggression perpetrated through technology. Cyberbullying is one type of electronic aggression. Brainstorm all the other types of electronic aggression. Ask if anyone in the class has experienced any acts of electronic aggression. Research legal consequences.

Each of us needs to decide how we want to react if we

experience an incident of bullying as a target or a witness. Discuss what options are available inside and outside the school. If there are no helpful options in your school, how can you and others make the school accountable?

If your school does not have a posted statement of respectful behavior, perhaps you and your friends could create one. Try publishing it in your school newspaper. One elementary school had this one-sentence creed: "We don't hurt anybody's insides or outsides."

Always remember to treat others with respect, and expect to be treated with respect.

Suicide

Suicide is the third leading cause of death in young people ages fifteen to twenty-four. Since 1992, suicide among youth has slowly declined, but the rates are still high. Why are people of this age so vulnerable to suicide?

If a friend told you he or she was thinking about suicide, what would you do? What resources do you know of in the school or outside?

Secrets keep us sick. Secrets stand in the way of healing. If a friend made you promise not to tell that he is thinking of committing suicide, would you keep your promise? Is it better to have a dead friend who still trusts you, or a live friend who is angry with you?

Daelyn was teased and bullied her whole life. Do you think there's anything she could have done differently to resolve the problem? Did adults let her down?

Some people contemplate suicide as a way to make their attackers feel guilty. Why isn't this a good plan?

Most young people who have considered suicide say they felt hopeless, or isolated, or insignificant. Have you ever felt like that? What did you do to change your feelings? What are some healthy coping behaviors? What are some unhealthy coping behaviors?

Suicide Warning Signs
(From National Suicide Prevention Lifeline)

* Threatening to hurt or kill oneself or talking about wanting to hurt or kill oneself

* Looking for ways to kill oneself by seeking access to firearms, available pills, or other means

* Talking or writing about death, dying, or suicide when these actions are out of the ordinary for the person

* Feeling hopeless

* Feeling rage or uncontrolled anger or seeking revenge

* Acting reckless or engaging in risky activities—seemingly without thinking

* Feeling trapped—like there's no way out

* Increasing alcohol or drug use

* Withdrawing from friends, family, and society

* Feeling anxious, agitated, or unable to sleep, or sleeping all the time

* Experiencing dramatic mood changes

* Seeing no reason for living or having no sense of purpose in life

If you hear or see someone you know exhibiting any of these signs, seek help immediately. Contact a mental health professional or call the National Suicide Prevention Lifeline at 1-800-273-TALK. It is better to be embarrassed than to do nothing and lose a friend. The most common emotion shared by those around someone who commits suicide is guilt.

Suicide Prevention Hotlines and Web Sites

We can all band together to help each other during the hard times in our lives. If you need to speak with a trained counselor through a telephone crisis hotline, please pick up the phone. Most hotlines are open 24 hours a day, 7 days a week. Don't be afraid. Everything you say is confidential.

National Suicide Hotline: 1-800-SUICIDE (784-2433)

National Suicide Prevention Lifeline: 1-800-273-TALK (273-8255)

Suicide Awareness Voices of Education: www.save.org

American Foundation for Suicide Prevention (AFSP):

1-888-333-AFSP (333-2377)

www.afsp.org

Adolescent Crisis Intervention & Counseling Nineline:
1-800-999-9999

Self-Injury Hotline: SAFE (Self Abuse Finally Ends) Alternatives
Program: www.selfinjury.com

1-800-DONT CUT (366-8288)

Youth America Hotline
Peer Counseling
1-877-Youthline (968-8454)

Anti-Bullying Hotlines and Web Sites

If you are being bullied, or would like to talk to a trained professional about your situation or that of a friend, there are anti-bullying crisis hotlines. Most are open 24 hours a day, 7 days a week. Everything you say will be kept confidential.

National Youth Violence Prevention Resource Center
www.safeyouth.org/scripts/topics/bullying.asp

Girls and Boys Town Hotline: 1-800-448-3000
www.boystown.org

Teen Helpline: 1-800-400-0900

The first Bullying and Cyberbullying sites:

swww.bullying.org

www.cyberbullying.org (also www.cyberbullying.ca)

Be Web Aware contains Internet safety tips for kids from two years to seventeen years in age.

http://www.bewebaware.ca

i-Safe educates students, school staff, and parents on Internet safety.

http://www.isafe.org

Wired Kids focuses on preventing cybercrimes and abuses.

www.wiredkids.org

International Sources

Suicide and Mental Health Association International:

www.suicideandmentalhealthassociationinternational.org/
Crisis.html

www.suicidehotlines.com/international.html

Anyone over age fifteen can become an activist for suicide prevention. For more information on training go to www.livingworks.net

And see: www.dmoz.org/Kids_and_Teens/Teen_Life/Suicide/

This guide was prepared by C. J. Bott, educational consultant and author of: *The Bully in the Book and the Classroom* (Scarecrow, 2004) and *More Bullies in More Books* (Scarecrow, 2009).

www.bulliesinbooks.com